Praise for
THE CAMPAIGN

"With the perfect bend of humor, drama, and
the secret inner workings of middle-school politics,
The Campaign has my vote!"

—*Brooks Benjamin, author of*
My Seventh-Grade Life in Tights

"Readers will root for ambitious Amanda Adams as she
mounts her campaign for seventh-grade class president—
and manages the unexpected drama of running against
her own best friend. Full of insider election details . . .
The Campaign is a fun, timely, and inspiring must-read
for politically engaged young readers."

—*Rebecca Behrens, author of* When Audrey Met Alice
and Alone in the Woods

"Middle-school friendship drama meets modern-day politics
in this timely, hilarious, and heartfelt story!"

—*Jen Malone, author of* The Sleepover

"*The Campaign* by Laurie Friedman is a joy to read!
A feel-good, quick-paced story of resilience . . . . You will root
hard for Amanda Adams, daughter of a congresswoman,
as she faces countless personal and political challenges
running for president of her seventh-grade class!"

—*Elizabeth Atkinson, award-winning author of*
I, Emma Freke; The Island of Beyond; *and* Fly Back, Agnes

The

CAMPAIGN

with
LIBERTY
and
STUDY HALL
FOR ALL

Laurie
Friedman

RP|KIDS
PHILADELPHIA

Running Press Kids
Hachette Book Group
1290 Avenue of the Americas, New York, NY 10104
www.runningpress.com/rpkids
@RP_Kids

Printed in the United States of America

First Edition: September 2020

Published by Running Press Kids, an imprint of Perseus Books, LLC, a subsidiary of Hachette Book Group, Inc. The Running Press Kids name and logo is a trademark of the Hachette Book Group.

The Hachette Speakers Bureau provides a wide range of authors for speaking events. To find out more, go to www.hachettespeakersbureau.com or call (866) 376-6591.

The publisher is not responsible for websites (or their content) that are not owned by the publisher.

Print book cover and interior design by Frances J. Soo Ping Chow

Library of Congress Control Number: 2019950313

ISBNs: 978-0-7624-9624-2 (hardcover), 978-0-7624-9625-9 (ebook)

LSC-C

10   9   8   7   6   5   4   3   2   1

For
BECCA AND ADAM.
WITH ALL MY HEART,
L.B.F.

A NOTE FROM THE AUTHOR:

Dear Reader,

I hope you enjoy reading about Amanda's campaign to be president of her class. In the story, Amanda's mother, a member of Congress, encourages Amanda to keep a notebook about past presidents of the United States to learn about ways in which they led our nation. As her mother points out, they all played a role in shaping our nation, but sometimes made decisions and acted in ways that were not in the best interest of all people. She encourages Amanda to focus on their accomplishments as a way to help her better understand how to be a good and effective leader. She also suggests that Amanda continue to study past presidents to gain a more complete and thorough understanding of their legacies and the role they played in the history of our nation. I hope each of you will do your own research that leads to a deeper, more comprehensive understanding of our nation's history.

Keep reading, keep learning, and most of all, enjoy *The Campaign*!

Laurie Friedman

Chapter One
A COZY DINNER FOR THREE

Amanda, please sit up straight."

My spine straightens instantly. Years of practice is my secret. Slouching at the Adams's family dinner table is *not* permitted. But reading the newspaper is. Same goes for eating takeout straight from the container. Mom spears a chunk of kung pao chicken with her chopsticks, then passes the front section of today's *Washington Post* to Dad. There's an article in it she wants him to see. I don't have to look to know it's about politics. In my house, it's *always* about politics.

Mom is a congresswoman from Virginia. The Honorable Carol Adams. She, Dad, and I live in Arlington, which is right across the Potomac River from Washington, D.C., where she works on Capitol Hill, doing her part to run our nation's government. My father, Harry, helps run *her*. That's their little inside joke about what he does. They think it's funny. I think it makes Mom sound like a puppy out for a morning walk.

But that's another story. About puppies. Okay. I won't make you wait for it.

Here's an important fact to know about me. My family is small. Just Mom, Dad, and me. No brothers. No sisters. Not even a dog or cat. I've tried everything I could think of to get a pet, even telling Mom her approval ratings would skyrocket if she was photographed holding a cute little furry puppy. I thought it was a genius plan. Too bad for me it didn't work. One thing I've learned over the years: some campaigns are more successful than others. But I haven't given up. One of my goals is to finish seventh grade with a puppy by my side.

My mantra: *I will get a puppy*.

Anyway, back to Dad. He has spent his entire professional life managing one political campaign after another to get my mom to where she is today. Now he runs her office. It's his job to make sure she's where she needs to be, saying what needs to be said, and looking good while she says it. That last part is important, at least to Mom. She's one of those never-a-hair-out-of-place types, especially if she's on camera or speaking in front of an audience. Which is most days. Dad's job also includes making sure all of the phone calls Mom receives (anywhere from a few to thousands in a single day) get answered and that her staff gives the right answers.

Even though my parents live together and work together, they never argue. *Almost never.* The only thing they ever argue about is who has the most important job. Dad says it's Mom. Mom swears it's Dad. Truth is, my parents are a dynamic duo that never quits. *Like now.*

They're both eating shrimp lo mein with chopsticks *while* reading the *Washington Post.* For an only child, that sounds like dinner might be a lonely time. *Au contraire.* (It's a term I learned in French class that means: nope, you got it wrong.) The great thing about parents who read during dinner is that they don't stop my under-the-table scrolling through Instagram or texting with my best friend, Meghan Hart.

> Amanda: Something BIG to tell you tomorrow!

> Meghan: What is it?! Tell me now.

> Amanda: ☺

> Meghan: KK. Something BIG to tell you too!

I pause and wonder what Meghan's big thing is. Could be she's getting her braces off, which I didn't think she needed in the first place. Meghan has naturally straight teeth and the biggest smile (even with braces on) of anyone at our school. Seriously, it's a thing. If there were a superlatives category in the yearbook for "Biggest Smile," Meghan would win.

And tomorrow, her smile will be bigger than ever when she hears what I have to say.

That's because it's life-changing stuff. Not just for me. For her, too. I really want to tell her now. But what I have to say is the sort of thing that's meant to be said in person.

Meghan knows I'm running for president of our seventh-grade class at Liberty Middle School. It's pretty much the only thing I've talked about for days now. But what Meghan doesn't know is that I'm planning to ask her to run as my vice president. Seriously, who else would I ask? I close my eyes and imagine her reaction. I see squealing. Screaming. Hop-around hugging. My fingers move like race cars nearing the finish line as I text her.

> Amanda: Meet me outside Mrs. Lee's class.

> Meghan: Before homeroom?

> Amanda: YES! NEWS Is BIG!

> Meghan: KK. CU then.☺

"Amanda, how was your day at school?" Mom asks.

My eyes shoot up from my phone. Apparently the *Washington Post* isn't as interesting as I thought it was. "Um . . . good . . . I mean . . . well, you see . . ." I fumble, suddenly unsure how to tell my parents the news I've been waiting all day (actually since last week) to share with them. It's not that I don't want to tell them; I just know they'll have a LOT to say on this topic.

They both narrow their eyes at me. I'm not a fumbler, and they know it.

Dad puts down his paper. "Amanda, what's going on?" he asks.

I chew on my lower lip and study Dad. The day I had to have emergency surgery to remove my appendix, he was a nine on the parental concern scale. When I wanted to go to the mall for the first time without him or Mom, and just Meghan, he was a six. As the child of a politician and a politician's chief strategist, I've learned to gauge people's reactions. Right now, the interest level in his voice is officially a four. But that can go up fast. There's no more delaying. I clear my throat. "I have an announcement to make . . ." My voice trails off. Dad's interest level in my life is about to go from four to TEN. Which isn't good.

"Amanda, spit it out!" Mom leans across the table toward me, like she can't wait another second. Patience was never her thing.

I tuck a long red curl behind my left ear. "I'm running for office," I tell my parents. "I want to be the next president of the seventh grade at Liberty Middle School."

The sound of chopsticks clattering to the table fills our dining room. Mom's and Dad's brows shoot up higher than the Washington Monument (which is 555 feet 5⅛ inches tall, to be exact).

"Amanda, that's wonderful news!" Mom flashes me her TV

smile. It's the one she gives to say she supports an idea. Like more affordable health care. She's big on that.

I look to Dad. When it comes to campaigns, he can't help himself. Dad is a planner, a strategist, an endless source of good advice. His wheels are spinning. I can see it.

"Amanda, first rule of a campaign: choose your words carefully," Dad says.

"Huh?" I ask, confused.

"Don't say you *want* to be the next president of the seventh grade. Say you're *going* to be the next president of the seventh grade," Dad says. "And you will be. Politics is in your DNA. Elections have been part of your life since you were a baby."

That much is true. The first word out of my mouth was *mama*. The second, *dada*. And the third, fourth, and fifth—*have you voted?* In preschool, my parents didn't read me books before bed. They told me stories of important political figures and how they made a difference. I went to kindergarten with buttons to give out, my mom's smiling face plastered all over them. I don't remember a time when she wasn't running for office and Dad wasn't planning a campaign to get her elected. So now it makes sense that I'm running for office, too.

"Amanda, you're going to make a wonderful president," Mom says.

"If you're going to run for president, you're going to need two things," adds Dad.

My brain reels with possibilities. *A new wardrobe. A smarter phone.*

But Dad says nothing about either. "The first thing you'll need is a running mate."

I roll my eyes. Dad knows there's only one person I would ever ask to be my vice president. "I'm going to ask Meghan."

Dad nods his approval, then moves on. "Next thing you'll need for a successful campaign is a notebook." He rises from his seat at the table and walks in the direction of the office he and Mom share. When he returns, he hands me a shiny red notebook. "The best politicians are informed ones. If you want to be president, you'll need to read and make notes about past presidents and what they've done to make a difference. Let them be your inspiration."

I bite my lip to keep from laughing out loud. Dad might know a thing or two about national politics. But middle school? Not so much.

"Um, Dad, I'm pretty sure no past presidents of the seventh grade at Liberty Middle School will provide the kind of inspiration you're talking about." I try to give him back the notebook. It's the last thing I need to get elected.

"Amanda, think big!" booms Mom. "Your father doesn't mean past presidents of the seventh grade at Liberty Middle School. He's talking about past presidents of the United States."

Now I can't help but laugh. On the dumb ideas scale, this

one is a ten.

"There's a lot you'll be surprised to learn about some of our past leaders," adds Mom, ignoring my laughter.

Um. Yeah. I'm sure there's a lot to learn about our nation's former presidents. But how it's going to help me get elected president of my class is a mystery.

I use my chopsticks to push aside chunks of red pepper and celery in search of any remaining chicken in my take-out carton. There isn't any, so I pop a peanut into my mouth and take my time chewing it. I'm entering dangerous territory with my parents and need to choose my words carefully.

"Knowing a few trivia facts isn't going to help me win my class election. You might think it will, but it won't."

"Amanda." My parents say my name together in their "we're the parents" voice, which is my least favorite of all their voices. It's just not fair, the whole two-on-one thing.

"Seriously, do I have to keep a notebook about past presidents?" I ask.

"Yes!" Two voices ring out as one.

"Amanda, all of our presidents played a role in shaping our nation. That doesn't mean they always made good decisions and acted in the best interest of all people. Focus on their accomplishments as a way to learn how to be a good and effective leader." Mom gives me an encouraging smile like I'm about to go on an interesting journey.

But I'm not so sure about that. Keeping a notebook about our presidents while trying to get elected myself isn't exactly a priority. Plus I have a big question. "There are like forty-something United States presidents," I remind my parents.

Dad makes a *tssk* sound. "Forty-five," he states, like I should know the exact number.

"Right." I shrug as though he's helped make my point. "So where would I even start?"

"That's simple," says Dad. "Always start at the beginning."

✳ ✳ ✳

MY CAMPAIGN INSPIRATION NOTEBOOK

I, Amanda Adams, am being forced to keep this silly notebook by my campaign-crazed parents who refuse to accept the fact that no one has ever been elected president of anything with the help of an inspiration notebook. But since I have no choice, here goes.

✳ George Washington ✳

BORN: February 22, 1732, Westmoreland County, Virginia
DIED: December 14, 1799, Mount Vernon, Virginia
SIGN: Pisces (Positive traits: imaginative, compassionate, intuitive. Negative traits: pessimistic, lazy, oversensitive.)
PARTY: Federalist (Huh? No one has ever even heard of that party.)
STATUS: Married to Martha Dandridge Washington

KIDS: None of his own; stepfather to Martha's two kids (John and Martha)

YEARS OF PRESIDENCY: 1789 to 1797

PRO: Good letter writer (he wrote over 20,000 of them)

CON: Owned slaves (this often gets glossed over)

NICKNAME: Father of His Country

FAVORITE FOOD: Hoe cakes (Like pancakes but made on the back of a hoe or a shovel. Look it up if you really want to know more.)

DOG OR CAT LOVER: DOGS!

✳ ✳ ✳

To be honest, if I could do it my way, I'd stop right here. But on the chance my parents snoop (and it's a high chance) to see what I've written, I know Mom and Dad will be looking for me to make some "deeper connections" about George's personality, background, and character that made him a good president. So without further ado . . . here are a few notebook-worthy facts about our nation's first president.

One: George Washington wasn't afraid of a little hard work.

His father died when he was eleven. He had some older stepbrothers, but they were off at school, so young George had no choice but to help out his mother at home. He went to a local school where math was his favorite subject. At fifteen, his formal education stopped, and at seventeen he was already working full time as a surveyor. (Something about land and maps. I'll save you the trouble of looking it up.) But in addition to being a farmer, then a soldier, then president, George spent his whole life continuing to read and learn.

Bottom line: If you want to be president, you have to be willing to work hard (ugh . . . I can't believe I'm about to write these next words) and be a lifelong learner.

Two: George Washington had good manners.

I know . . . who cares how he held his fork? But it was more than that. At age fourteen, young George wrote out a copy of *110 Rules of Civility and Decent Behavior in Company and Conversation.* These were some very old rules written in France in 1595. But honestly, some of the stuff they had to say (even though they said it in a really old-fashioned, stuffy sort of way) still makes sense today.

Like *do not laugh too loud or too much at a public spectacle.* And *be not apt to relate news if you know not the truth thereof.* In other words, don't laugh at people when they do something dumb and don't gossip. Apparently, George lived his whole life according to these rules and was known for trying to be a gentleman.

Bottom line: Not a bad idea to be well-behaved if you want to be president.

Three: George Washington was all about the future.

He was a commander in the army that fought hard (and for a long time) in the war against the British. Why? Because he saw a brighter future for America. He also presided over the Constitutional Convention. No doubt, that was a lot of work, but George did it because it was important to him to come up with a way of governing our country that would make sense for generations to come. He was president TWICE! That's right. He did such a fine job the first go-round that he was reelected, and the second time, he spent a lot of his time in office making sure our nation (which back then was just the states on the East Coast) grew and expanded west.

Why? Because he believed the future of our nation was all about growing it from small and powerless to BIG AND POWERFUL!

> **Bottom line: Being a leader means doing things that make your country (or in my case, my grade) better than it was before you took office.**

> *Four: George Washington wore a lot of hats*

I know. In all those old pictures, he always has on that dark funny-looking one.

But what I mean is that he played a lot of roles. In addition to being our nation's first president, he was a son, a brother, a husband, a father, a grandfather, an army commander, a surveyor, a land owner, a planter, a hoe-cake eater, a letter writer, and . . . wait for it (because this is the big finale) . . . George Washington was a dog lover. He had more than thirty of them! In fact, some things I read said that he had as many as fifty dogs in his lifetime. That's a lot of dogs!

> **Bottom line: If you want to get elected president, GET A DOG! Or fifty of them.**

• •

Dear Mom and Dad,

If you read this (which I have a feeling you will), I need a dog. Our nation's first president had a whole bunch, and he got elected to office twice. All I need is one! Do your part to help me get elected. Please get me a dog!

Love,
Amanda

P.S. The election is right around the corner, so there's no time to waste!!!

• •

Chapter Two

DRUMROLL, PLEASE!

Amanda, move it!"

The *clickety-clack* of Mom's heels impatiently tapping against the brick foyer by the front door drifts up the stairs and into my room. She's got places to be, people to see, things to do. I get that. But today is a big day for me, too. I take my time smearing my lips with Cherry Sugar lip gloss, the new color Meghan and I bought at the mall last weekend, then look into the mirror over my dresser to inspect the result. Little flecks of red, pink, and gold shimmer up at me. I sniff the air. Mmmm! Cherry Sugar smells as good as it looks.

"AMANDA!" On the impatience scale, Mom is officially a nine.

"Coming," I yell. I pull on my new hoodie, the cute pink one that Meghan spent most of last Saturday helping me find. I told her I needed just the right article of clothing to announce my candidacy as class president, and this hoodie is perfect! It says GIRL POWER on the back and screams "leader." Just what I need for today. I grab my backpack and head downstairs.

Mom herds me out the door like a stray sheep. She shoves a protein bar into one of my hands and a water bottle into the other. In case you had any illusions that she's the kind of parent who wakes up and makes pancakes shaped like Mickey Mouse ears, with chopped fresh fruit on the side, let me dispel them here and now. She's not. Neither is Dad. He's already in the driver's seat with the motor running. I close the door behind me and start on my breakfast. It's a short drive to Liberty Middle, which means I have to eat fast.

"Good morning," Dad says in his "Mom and I have important business today" voice.

They're not the only ones. "This morning I'm going to make my candidacy for seventh-grade president official," I inform my parents. Dad glances in the rearview mirror, waiting for me to elaborate. "In homeroom, Mrs. Lee is passing out the forms for anyone who wants to run. All I have to do is to fill it out and, voilà, I'll be a candidate," I explain.

Mom turns around and gives me a thumbs-up. "Amanda, I'm thrilled for you. Declaring your candidacy is the first step of any campaign. And it's an important one. The declaration of your candidacy sets the tone for the rest of your campaign. It's critical that you show your constituents who you are and what kind of a leader you'll be."

"Yep. I'm on it," I say to Mom, who is sort of overthinking this whole running-for-president-of-my-class thing. It's not exactly like running for the United States Congress. And over half of the seventh grade went to elementary school with me. People know me.

But declaring my candidacy is only one thing on my agenda today.

The other is talking to Meghan. Dad pulls into the drop-off lane and my stomach rumbles. It's a mix of water, protein bar, and anticipation. Minutes from now I'm going to secure my vice president, then after that we'll tell the rest of the world, or at least everyone in our grade, our plan to become their class leaders. I hop out of the car, charge through the doors of the school, and hurry toward the area outside Mrs. Lee's room, where Meghan and I agreed to meet.

I see her from a distance and wave, hurrying in her direction. I'm practically bursting to talk to her. When I get to her, my mouth falls open, but no words come out of it.

Meghan has a new haircut.

"Wow!" I say. Her thick brown hair has been cut into shoulder-length layers. Not the kind that just hang around your face. She has the kind that actually make a face look better than it would without them. Like Roxie Scott, the weather lady on TV. "You look amazing," I add. "I didn't know you were getting your hair cut. That must have been your big news."

Meghan smiles, but it isn't her normal, extra-big smile. It's actually kind of small.

"Um, not exactly," says Meghan.

Then I notice something else. In addition to her new haircut, Meghan has on a sweater I've never seen before. Sparkly silver. With cool new sneaks to match. I zip my GIRL POWER hoodie to my chin. Somehow it doesn't seem as cute now as it did this morning. I take the ponytail holder from my wrist and wind it around my curls to make them neat, like Meghan's sleek new do. Suddenly, I have this bad feeling, like maybe I should find out Meghan's news before I tell her my own. "So what's your big news?" I ask.

Meghan shifts from one foot to the other. "You first," she says.

"You," I say.

"No, you," she shoots back.

We giggle at the same time.

"Okay. Rock, Paper, Scissors," says Meghan. "Three rounds. Winner goes second."

We both stick out our hands. Round one goes to me. Rounds two and three to Meghan, which means it's my turn to talk. I clear my throat. "Drumroll, please."

Meghan pats her hands against her thighs.

"You know how I told you I'm going to run for president of

our class?" I wait, but Meghan doesn't answer. She just makes an *mmm-hmm* sound, so I continue. "Well, I wanted to know if you want to run with me. As my vice president. It'll be amazing! You and I will be in charge of the whole grade, which means we get to plan the community service project our class does *and* pick the theme for the seventh-grade dance in the spring. How fun does that sound?"

I exhale, equal parts relieved and mad at myself for being nervous in the first place. There's only one answer Meghan could possibly have. I flash her my biggest smile and wait for it. We both take French, so it's possible her answer will be *"Oui! Oui!"*

"Well . . . you see . . . I . . . um . . ." Meghan sounds like I did last night when I was having trouble telling Mom and Dad that I'm running. I fumbled and I'm not a fumbler. One of the many things Meghan and I have in common is that she isn't, either.

On the alarmed scale, I'm a six. "You want to be my vice president, don't you?"

Meghan shakes her new layers off her face. Are there highlights in them? I'm sure I see an unmistakable strand of blond.

"Amanda . . . you see . . . the thing I wanted to tell you is that . . ."

Whatever it is, I'm pretty sure she doesn't want to tell me. "Meghan, spit it out!" I know I sound just like Mom. But I can't help it. I'm her daughter, after all, and I have to know. *NOW!*

Meghan puts her shoulders back. The first bell rings. Kids

are walking into their homerooms and giving us funny looks. I stand there, waiting for Meghan to tell me her news.

"Girls, are you coming?" Mrs. Lee is holding the door open for us to walk inside.

Neither of us move. I glance at Mrs. Lee. Her face squishes up like she senses something is off. A cold fall breeze cuts through the warmth of my hoodie. Every morning, Meghan and I are always the first ones in Mrs. Lee's classroom. That's because we **LOVE** homeroom.

We **LOVE** that we have Mrs. Lee as our advisor. Not only is she the coolest teacher at Liberty Middle School, but she also teaches science, which Meghan and I have together fifth period. It's our favorite class. We both **LOVE** science and doing experiments in Mrs. Lee's lab.

And we **LOVE** that we have the same homeroom and get to start every day together.

When Meghan and I got our schedules at the beginning of the year, we squealed like our celeb crushes (mine is Shawn Mendes and hers is Harry Styles, who she likes a lot, but not nearly as much as her real crush, quarterback of the football team and eighth-grade uber hottie Caleb Johannsen) had handed them to us.

"Meghan, we have homeroom AND lunch AND Science AND French together!" I said.

"That's so cool!" said Meghan, then she blushed. "I heard

Caleb is switching from Spanish to French this year. What if he has French with us?!?"

We both squealed some more at the possibility that Meghan might have a class with her crush. He's the hottest guy in the eighth grade, and Meghan is always talking about him. Literally, we've spent whole sleepovers discussing his blue eyes and how they sparkle like swimming pools on a sunny day. Of course, I've been sworn to absolute secrecy to never tell anyone how Meghan feels about Caleb. Which I would never do. One: because Meghan is my best friend. And two: because on the secret scale, this one is a ten. Meghan would die of embarrassment if anyone besides me knew how she felt.

Mrs. Lee motions to us to come inside the classroom. "Girls, let's go."

Every single morning since the school year started, Meghan and I have raced into her classroom ahead of everyone else so we can grab the two desks right in front of hers. We always squish them so close together that Mrs. Lee jokes we're like twins joined at the hip, except that we're joined by desks. But now, we just stand there, neither of us moving a muscle.

"So, do you or don't you want to be my vice president?" I ask, silently willing Meghan to go with the *do* option.

She sighs. "Amanda, I can't be your vice president."

Light bounces off a sparkly patch on Meghan's sweater and I blink. "Why not?" I ask.

Meghan's cheeks turn pink as she answers. "Because I'm running for president of the seventh grade, too."

"What?" I'm confused. Then it hits me like a soccer ball aimed straight at my head. My best friend isn't going to be my vice president. She's going to be my opponent.

Chapter Three
A HISTORY LESSON
(BUT NOT ABOUT U.S. PRESIDENTS)

At this point, you might be asking yourself some pretty big questions.

Like when and why and how did Amanda Elizabeth Adams and Meghan Louise Hart come to be best friends? And if they're such good friends, how is it possible that Meghan decided to run for president of the seventh grade at Liberty Middle School when Amanda had already told her she was running?

Well, that last one is a great question.

In fact, as Amanda sits in Mrs. Lee's homeroom listening to her explain how to fill out the form stating one's intent to run for class president, she's asking herself that same thing.

It makes absolutely NO sense to Amanda why Meghan would do that!

She searches her brain for an answer, but can't think of one, so she turns her attention to the other question. The one about when and why and how she and Meghan became friends.

That question is much simpler for her to answer.

Amanda Elizabeth Adams and Meghan Louise Hart became best friends on the first moment of the first day of first grade at Patriot Elementary when Mrs. Hudson lined up her class alphabetically. Amanda was at the front of the line because her last name is Adams and Meghan was somewhere in the middle because her last name is Hart. But Meghan didn't want to be in the middle, so she offered Amanda a quarter, two purple marbles, and a snack-sized Kit Kat (left over from the previous Halloween) to switch places with her. Amanda said she'd do it, but only if Meghan gave her the Hello Kitty Watch on her wrist. Meghan took it off, Amanda put it on, and the two switched spots in line. From that moment on, they were BFFs.

That's the short answer. Now here's the Wikipedia version.

WIKIPEDIA
THE FREE ENCYCLOPEDIA

The Friendship of Amanda and Meghan

How It Started

Amanda Adams and Meghan Hart became best friends in Mrs. Hudson's first-grade class at Patriot Elementary School. Their relationship was described as one that got off to a rocky start. Day one, Amanda and Meghan got into a fight. Something about a watch. Meghan claimed it was hers. Amanda said Meghan gave it to her. They were pulling and tugging the watch back and forth like they were playing a game of tug-of-war. And they were yelling things like "It's mine!" and "No, it's mine!" when Mrs. Hudson said, "The watch is mine. At least for now." She took it and put Amanda and Meghan together in the time-out corner. When twenty minutes (the official length of Patriot Elementary School time-outs) had passed, they were both smiling (their faces covered in chocolate from the Kit Kat bar they'd shared) and chatting so much that Mrs. Hudson threatened to put them right back in time-out if they couldn't be quiet.

The Early Years

Throughout elementary school, Amanda and Meghan's friendship strengthened. In second grade they made a pact to eat one food every day that turned their tongues blue or purple. If their mothers said anything like "No more popsicles!" the girls would politely remind them that they had to eat the popsicles because they'd made a pact. In third grade, Amanda and Meghan made a girl cave under Meghan's bed and used it for all sorts of things. Telling scary stories. Eating potato chips before dinner. And quietly hiding Amanda there when it was time for her to go home. They had sleepovers every weekend of fourth grade. And in fifth grade, they formed a running club (they were the only members) and decided to run a marathon. Their training started with one lap around Amanda's block. Then two. Once, they made it six times around, but when Amanda's dad told them that once around their Arlington block was 0.3 miles, they did the math and realized they would have to run around it 87.3 times to equal a whole marathon. So they switched their running club to a TV-watching club.

Off to Middle School

Sixth grade was a new adventure for Amanda and Meghan. They started Liberty Middle School and grew in what Amanda's mother called "natural different directions." Whatever that means. Point is, Amanda loved sports and made the soccer team. Meghan, who could sing before she talked (at least that's what she'd always claimed about herself) was cast as the lead in the sixth-grade play. That year, they spent time apart. Sometimes it worried Amanda that maybe it was a sign of things to come. But when Amanda asked her father if he believed in signs, he said, "No, only polls. And even those aren't always accurate." So Amanda disregarded any and all signs, and off she went, along with Meghan, to seventh grade.

The Here and Now

For the two friends, the school year started pretty well (in Amanda's opinion). She and Meghan had homeroom, lunch, Science, and French together. There were classes they didn't have together. And Amanda was still on the soccer team. She had practice every day after school while Meghan was off at drama club. That meant there were times Meghan couldn't have told Amanda something BIG (like that she was planning to run against her for president of their class!). But there were plenty of other opportunities when she could have told her. Like every day during homeroom, lunch, Science, or French. Or every night when they talked or texted. But Meghan never said a word. On the contrary, Amanda only found out this very morning when she asked Meghan to be her vice president and a "highlighted-and-layered-haired, sparkly sweatered, and cool sneaks wearing" version of Meghan told Amanda she was running against her.

In homeroom, Amanda filled out the student government form her favorite teacher gave her and under the question *Why do you think you'd make a good president of the seventh grade?* Amanda didn't write the answer she'd planned to write, which was: *Because my best friend Meghan Hart is running with me as vice president and we always have the BEST ideas, which means things like the community service project and the seventh-grade dance will be more amazing than ever.* Instead, she gripped her pencil so tight it left a mark on her finger and wrote: *Because I have the BEST ideas, which means things like the community service project and the seventh-grade dance will be more amazing than ever.* And when she got to the question *Who will be your VP running mate?* she wrote: *TBD.* When she handed the form to Mrs. Lee, Amanda asked if she could get back to her on the question of who her vice president would be. Mrs. Lee gave her a smile (the kind you give a person who you feel sorry for) and told her she could have until the end of the week to let her know her answer.

Then Amanda turned and looked at Meghan, who was sitting in a desk in the last row of the classroom, next to Bree Simon. And she was smiling as she handed her own form to Mrs. Lee. Amanda tried to make eye contact with Meghan—something she'd done hundreds of times before. Always when she did, Meghan made eye contact back like she knew, in the way only a best friend could, that Amanda wanted her attention. But this time, Meghan didn't know. Or pretended not to. Either way, she didn't make eye contact back with Amanda. Then Mrs. Lee asked for all eyes on her and made a few more announcements before homeroom ended. When it did, Amanda hurried out of the classroom. Partly because she had first-period Algebra with Mr. Corbett, whose classroom was all the way across campus, which meant she had to hurry to get there in time. But also because she was scared that if she waited, Meghan would walk out of homeroom with Bree. Amanda wanted to talk to Meghan about what happened, but she didn't want to talk to Meghan AND Bree. And without looking behind her as she left homeroom, she had a bad feeling they would be together.

So . . . Amanda walked alone to first-period Algebra and her brain filled with questions.

Questions like: What in the world made Meghan decide to run for president when she knew that meant they would be running against each other? Did Meghan change her hair and get new clothes because she wanted to look extra good to announce that she was running for president of their grade? Why did she sit next to Bree Simon in homeroom? Like, what did Bree Simon have to do with things? And most important, how were she and Meghan supposed to keep being best friends now that they were opponents, too?

Chapter Four

THE PROBLEM WITH CINNAMON ROLLS

(OR, WHY THIS WEDNESDAY I'M TOTALLY NOT IN THE MOOD FOR MINE)

My eyes dart around the cafeteria looking for Meghan. And Jen. And Jill. And Jayda. Since the start of seventh grade, they've been my B-schedule lunch buddies. Normally, I don't have to look for them. Especially on Cinnamon Roll Wednesdays.

Wednesdays are when the cafeteria at Liberty Middle School serves breakfast for lunch. Eggs. Bacon. Hash browns. And cinnamon rolls. Ooey, gooey, warm, and yummy cinnamon rolls! Meghan and the J's (that's what Jen, Jill, and Jayda are officially called) and I all LOVE Cinnamon Roll Wednesdays. We're always at the head of the line so we're first to get our breakfast for lunch, then go right to our seats and gobble it up.

But today, there's no sign of Meghan. Or Jen. Or Jill. Or Jayda.

Ben Ball, class clown and stand-up comedian wannabe (but ain't gonna be), is behind me and gives a little kick to the back of my ankle.

"Grab a tray, Adams, and move on. Or move out." He snort-laughs like his joke was funny. Which it wasn't. Meghan and I never laugh at his jokes because they're not funny, but also because if you laugh at even one of them, Ben Ball follows you around, snort-laughing and telling you another and another and another joke until you want to scream, "BEN BALL, STOP TELLING ME JOKES OR I'M GOING TO SCREAM!" But today, I turn around.

"Ha, ha." I fake-laugh, then take a tray and move up into the line.

Ben takes his own tray and shoves it onto the sliding rails so it bumps against mine. "Suddenly you think my jokes are funny?" He sniffs the air like he smells something other than warm cinnamon. "Buttering me up, eh? Trying to get my vote. Heard you're running for class president. Is it true, Adams? You'd make a good president, you know."

"Um, thanks," I say, surprised at how fast word travels around here.

"So where's your posse?" he asks.

Meghan. The J's. *My posse.* I scan the cafeteria again, but no sign of them anywhere. "Running late. They'll be here," I say, hopeful I sound more confident than I feel.

Ben snort-laughs. "Not so sure about that," he says. "Wanna know what I heard?"

I'm pretty sure I don't.

I stare into the hairnet of the cafeteria lady who is scooping scrambled eggs onto plates and passing them along to the guy (also wearing a hairnet) in charge of hash browns. What could Ben have heard? Is it even possible that, only three periods later, the fact that Meghan is running against me for class president has already become newsworthy?

My stomach churns, but not from hunger. "Um, what'd you hear?" I finally ask.

Ben gives me a friendly clap on the back. "Now you want to be friends, too, huh?"

I don't answer. At least, not right away. The lady at the end of the line, the one in charge of doling out the cinnamon rolls, puts one on my plate and hands it to me.

"Gave you a big one," she says with a smile. "I know how much you and your friends like them. Then she looks down the line like she was expecting my normal gang of girls to be right behind me. Not Ben Ball. When she sees they're not, she leans forward and whispers, "I hear there's a virus going around."

It's almost like she doesn't want me to feel bad that they're not there. *Which makes me feel worse.* I thank her, take a carton of milk, and move out of the line.

"C'mon, Adams, you can sit with me," Ben says. "I'll spill the tea."

He shoots me a smug smile. But one last look around the cafeteria confirms what I already suspected: my friends are nowhere in sight. I walk with Ben to a table. He sits, then stuffs a whole slice of bacon into his mouth. When he's done chewing, he looks at me. "So, you want the whole truth and nothing but the truth? Or the sugarcoated version?"

Neither option seems great.

"Let's go with full truth," Ben says before I have a chance to answer. "Rumor has it there's a *coup* in the hen house."

"A what?" I ask.

Ben shakes his head at me. "You take French. You know what a coup is, don't you?"

"Yeah," I say. "It's when power is seized. Like from a government. But what does it have to do with a hen house?" I don't wait for Ben to explain. Whatever it is, it doesn't sound good. I lean across the table. "What's going on?" I ask, dreading Ben's answer.

Ben leans across the table, and I catch a whiff of bacon and body odor.

"I was in the office third period and heard Principal Ferguson tell Coach Cook that there are only three candidates running for seventh-grade president," Ben says. "You. Meghan. And Frankie Chang. You know . . . the kid who should be in fourth grade but is so smart he finished third and skipped straight to seventh."

I raise a brow. "Frankie Chang skipped three grades?"

Ben clacks his teeth together. The sound makes me want to get up from the table and run. "Maybe it was two. Or one." Ben waves a hand through the air. "I don't know exactly how many grades the boy skipped. The details of Frankie Chang's academic record aren't what matters."

There's a long pause.

"Adams, you're going to be running against a prepubescent math genius and your best friend, or, I should say, former best friend." He clamps his lips together like he's waiting for the words to sink in, then says, "There's more. And you might not like it. I also heard Principal Ferguson tell Coach Cook that Meghan picked Bree Simon to be her running mate."

The cinnamon roll on my plate morphs into a giant, icing-covered lump of clay. Meghan is running against me! And she picked Bree Simon to be her vice president!

Bree Simon!?! Beautiful, cool, popular, superstar of the girls' basketball team Bree Simon!? She's Meghan's vice president? COULD THINGS BE ANY WORSE?!?

"Yes!" says Ben like he's reading my mind. "Things are much worse than they appear. Meghan has also picked her campaign staff. Your lunch buddies, otherwise known as the J's, are all going to be campaigning for the incomparable Miss Meghan H. and Baby Bree.

The way Ben says their names makes them sound more like rap stars than potential class officers. I shake my head like I've heard enough, but Ben keeps talking.

"That's right, Adams. The ladies who lunch with you . . . the ones who always eat their cinnamon rolls inside at the table in the corner . . . are sitting on the outside benches eating the lunches they brought from home. And who are they eating them with? Baby Bree herself."

The cafeteria spins around me and I grip the edges of the table.

At least now I know why Meghan and Jen, Jill, and Jayda aren't here. But it doesn't make it any better. Meghan running for president against me. Picking Bree as her veep. Eating lunch with her. Asking the J's to campaign for her. This is all a mistake.

A HUGE MISTAKE!

When I woke up this morning, I was so excited about the day ahead. I thought for sure Meghan and I would be spending it making plans for our campaign. Now all I want to do is talk to her and straighten out this whole mess.

I remember what Dad said last night when I told him I was going to run for president.

"Don't say you want *to be the next president of the seventh*

grade. *Say you're* going *to be the next president of the seventh grade.*"

I don't just *want* to straighten this out with Meghan.

I'm *going* to straighten it out!

"Um, Adams." Ben waves his hands in front of my face like he's trying to get my attention. "I don't know where your head is, but it needs to be thinking about who you're going to ask to be your vice president." He sits straighter. "I'm available. And you know what they say: everyone likes a funny candidate."

I wrinkle my nose at Ben. "I've never heard that."

He flashes me a smile, this one so big I can actually see his back teeth.

"Stick with me, Adams, and I'll teach you all sorts of things," Ben says. "How about this one: Why'd the vice president cross the road?"

But I miss the delivery of Ben's punch line.

Right now, I don't have time for jokes. I look at the big clock on the cafeteria wall. Lunches at Liberty Middle School are short. They fly by fast, but there's still eight minutes left of this one. Just enough time for me to go talk to Meghan.

And straighten this whole mess out.

Chapter Five
SMACKDOWN
(OR, IT'S A FREE COUNTRY. HAVEN'T YA HEARD?)

I march out of the cafeteria, past the outdoor picnic tables filled with students eating their lunches, laughing, and talking. I don't stop until I get to the one where Meghan, Jen, Jill, and Jayda are sitting with Bree and sharing a bag of apple slices with caramel dip.

I didn't even know Meghan liked caramel dip. *Not the point.* I'm here because I have something I need to say. And the sooner the better. I just want this whole mess straightened out.

I clear my throat and five sets of eyes (two blue, one hazel, and two brown) stare up at me. My stomach does a weird little flip. Then a flop.

"Um, can I talk to you?" I ask Meghan.

Her eyes flash with an emotion I can't quite put my finger

on. "Sure," she says, but she just keeps sitting there on the bench like whatever I have to say can be said in front of Jen, Jill, Jayda, and Bree.

I take a deep breath. "Alone?"

Meghan gives Bree this weird glance, almost like she's a student asking a teacher for permission to leave class and go to the bathroom. When Bree nods, Meghan stands up and we move a few feet away from their lunch table.

I look right at Meghan. "So, I'm not really sure what happened this morning."

Meghan shakes her hair off her face. "What do you mean?"

I feel a flash of anger. Meghan knows exactly what I mean. "Well, you knew I was running for president. So, I'm kind of surprised you decided to run, too." I pause, then continue. "And that you didn't tell me."

"I *did* tell you," Meghan shoots at me.

"Yeah. This morning," I shoot back. "You told me you were running for president only *after* I asked you if you wanted to be my vice president."

Meghan's hands are on her hips. "I texted you last night that I had something to tell you."

I can feel Bree, Jen, Jill, and Jayda watching us, but I block them out. Dad always says a good politician knows when to change tactics. I'm pretty sure now is a good time to change mine. I go with a softer approach.

"Meghan, what I'm trying to say is that I was really excited to ask you to be my vice president. I think we'd make a great team." I pause, carefully choosing the right words. "You're my best friend. I mean, all you have to do is say you want to be my vice president. I still really want you to be." I give her my friendliest smile. "So, do you wanna be?"

Meghan just stands there, chewing on her lip. That's something she does when she can't decide what she wants to say.

"What?" I ask, willing her to say what I want to hear.

"Amanda." Meghan says my name like she's talking in slo-mo. "I'm sorry."

She actually kind of looks it. But that doesn't make me feel any better. It's suddenly way too hot inside my GIRL POWER hoodie, and I unzip it. "I don't get it," I say.

Meghan's eyes laser focus on my hoodie. "Remember last weekend at the mall . . . all you wanted to do was shop for the perfect outfit to announce you were running for president?"

I nod, unsure where she's going with this.

"All day, *all* we did was shop for you."

A memory pops into my head—a memory of Meghan telling me she was starving and wanted to go to the food court and me telling her we had MUCH more important things to do. If I could push a do-over button and make our day at the mall include lunch, I would. But I can't.

"I'm sorry about that, Meghan. Really sorry." I push a

stray hair off my face. "But still, does it mean you have to run against me?"

Meghan just shrugs.

So that's her answer. Even though all she's doing is standing there in front of me, I feel like she just punched me in the gut. HARD! And it makes me want to punch back.

"So, were you going to tell me that you picked Bree Simon to be your vice president?" I ask, my voice louder than I intended. I motion to Jen, Jill, and Jayda. "Or that you asked them to work on your campaign? I mean, how long have you been planning this?"

Meghan narrows her eyes at me. "How'd you know that?"

My mouth falls open. "Does it really matter?"

Meghan huffs out loud like she's the one who has the right to be mad. I smell caramel. And apples. "Amanda, for the past week, all you've talked about is what *you* want. How *you* want to run for class president. How *you* want to be in charge of the community service project and the dance. How you needed the perfect outfit for today. I mean, honestly, I think you're being kind of . . . what's the word for it?" She chews on her bottom lip. "Selfish. It's all about you. But what if I want to be president, too?"

On the mad scale, I shoot straight to ten. How can Meghan call me selfish? Me telling her I want to be president and do things like plan the community service project or the dance isn't any different than her talking for weeks and weeks (which she did!) about auditioning for the school play and wanting to get the lead. Or talking until my ears go numb about how cute Caleb Johannsen is or what she can do to get him to notice her. And I can't think of one other day at the mall (and we've had lots of them) when it was all about me.

"I didn't even know you wanted to be president. Because you never said anything!" I say.

Meghan lets out a loud huff. "Well, now I have."

"We can't both be president." My voice is louder than I intended it to be.

"SMACKDOWN!" a boy yells from the next table.

I feel my face turning redder than my hair. I don't want to be having a fight with my best friend. Especially not with everyone watching like it's some kind of reality show. We've never even had a fight, which means I have no clue how to fight with her.

"I just think best friends shouldn't run against each other," I say, taking a reasonable approach. "Wouldn't it be great if one of us was president and one was vice president?"

Meghan picks a nonexistent piece of lint off her sweater. "Sure," she says. "But I don't want to be vice president."

Neither do I.

The wheels in my brain are going round and round, faster than a moving fidget spinner, as I piece this all together. Meghan knew I was running. Then decided to run and didn't tell me. Even worse, she cut her hair and bought new clothes and picked a vice president and a campaign team. ALL BEHIND MY BACK! If you ask me, that's *wrong*. **Wrong! Wrong! Wrong!**

"Did you ever think about the fact that it's a free country?" Meghan asks before I have a chance to say that I think the whole way she has gone about this is wrong. "Anyone can run for office. And I'm running for president of our class."

"Go Meghan!" Jayda makes a fist pump in the air.

"May the best candidate win," I snap.

What I don't say: that candidate is going to be me!

✳ ✳ ✳

MY CAMPAIGN INSPIRATION NOTEBOOK

✳ Thomas Jefferson ✳

BORN: April 13, 1743, Shadwell, Virginia

DIED: July 4, 1826 (50 years after the Declaration of Independence was signed!)

SIGN: Aries (Positive traits: adventurous, courageous, positive. Negative traits: arrogant, stubborn, and confrontational.)

POLITICAL PARTY: Democratic Republican (sounds confusing, but that's what the Democratic Party used to be called)

STATUS: Married to Martha (same name, different Martha than GW's) Skelton Jefferson

CON: Owned slaves: (guess independence only went so far)

NICKNAME: Father of the University of Virginia (that means he started it)

YEARS OF PRESIDENCY: 1801–1809

NUMBER OF LANGUAGES SPOKEN: 6

NUMBER OF LETTERS WRITTEN: 19,000

NUMBER OF BOOKS COLLECTED: 6,487

FAMOUS QUOTE: "I cannot live without books."

HOBBIES: Inventing, mockingbird keeping, astronomy, architecture, violin playing, gardening, math, fossil hunting, and (obviously) book collecting

✳ ✳ ✳

I'll admit that when Mom and Dad first suggested I keep a presidential inspiration notebook, I thought it was a pretty lame idea. But after what happened at school today, I'm kind of like . . . *Uh, yeah. I can use all the help I can get!* I mean, how could Meghan have decided to run against me without talking to me? Not to mention picking Bree to be her vice president and asking the J's to work on her campaign. The whole thing stinks (worse than Ben Ball). But I don't want to think about Meghan or Bree or the J's or Ben. Right now, it's all about TJ. Hopefully, our nation's third president and one of the authors of the Declaration of Independence can provide some serious inspo because I, Amanda Elizabeth Adams, need it!!! Okay. Here goes.

> *One: Thomas Jefferson was all about serving his country.*

He was president, vice president, secretary of state, and a congressman. He was governor of his home state, Virginia, where he also served in the legislature and held a bunch of other offices, too. Like seriously, he served his country and state for over fifty years.

> **Bottom line: TJ was committed. SO AM I! But is Meghan?!? It's kind of weird she never told me she had an interest in running for president. What made her decide she wanted to be president? Is she committed like TJ? Like me? Or is she in it for a different reason?**

Hmmm . . . something to think about. But not right now.

Two: Thomas Jefferson was an author.

At age thirty-three, he was one of the youngest delegates to the Second Continental Congress in Philadelphia, and he was appointed to a committee of five people to draft the Declaration of Independence. In case you're not sure what the Declaration is all about, Google it. But if you're too lazy or too busy or your mom took away your cell phone or your brother or sister is hogging the computer, trust me when I tell you it's probably the most important document about human rights ever written. It's the one that says: "all men are created equal."

> **Bottom line: Equality is big. And important. Like brushing your teeth before bed. Or sleeping in on Saturdays. Except it's even bigger and more important than either of those things.**

SOOOO . . . if all men (and women) are created equal, doesn't that make owning slaves wrong? Easy answer . . . YES!

Three: Thomas Jefferson was seriously into science.

As a kid, he liked to explore the land and learn about all of the natural wonders in the world around him. As an adult, he was a scholar in lots of scientific areas. Math. Botany. Medicine. Astronomy. Archaeology. Meteorology. Agriculture. And surveying. (What is with these presidents and their land and maps?!)

> **Bottom line: TJ and I have something in common. We both love science. Maybe that makes me a good candidate for president??? But it means Meghan is a good candidate, too. She likes science as much as I do. UGGH! My quest for inspiration continues . . .**

> *Four: Thomas Jefferson stood up for what he believed in.*

Like really stood up. TJ went on a hunger strike to show support for the citizens of Boston when the British government closed the Boston Harbor in response to the Boston Tea Party. That story is kind of long and too much to write about here, but the point is that he stopped eating and asked others to join him.

> **Bottom line: It's cool that TJ was into that "one for all and all for one" sort of thing, but I don't think asking the citizens of Liberty Middle to go on a hunger strike will get me elected.**

> *Five: Thomas Jefferson's face is on a lot.*

His face (and it's a pretty serious one) is on every nickel out there and on the two-dollar bill. There's even a memorial for him in Washington, D.C. And the memorial isn't just about his face. Inside, there's a nineteen-foot statue of his whole body made of pure bronze!

That's it! The inspiration I'm looking for! My face needs to be EVERYWHERE. On posters all over Liberty Middle School. I even have an idea for a campaign slogan: "Face It. Amanda Adams Is the Best Choice for President!"

I can see it! I'll make buttons that look like nickels with my face on them instead of Thomas Jefferson's. My heart beats faster in my chest. The good kind of faster, like I'm excited about something. For the first time all day, I feel like my campaign is finally on the right track.

Then, just as quickly as that good feeling arrived, it disappears. Is your first idea for a campaign slogan your best idea? Or should you brainstorm dozens of them? And what's the point of even thinking about slogans or buttons when I still don't have the main thing I need to run . . .

A vice president!

Chapter Six
WAKE UP AND SMELL THE HOT CHOCOLATE

I blink open my eyes and look at the clock on my nightstand. It's only 5:32 a.m. Officially, I don't have to be up for another fifty-eight minutes. But I have a big decision to make. *Who is going to be my vice president?* Since I can't count on Meghan, I need to find the right person for the job. Mrs. Lee says I have until the end of the week to make my decision. Today is Thursday, which means I don't have time to waste.

I throw back my covers and hop out of bed. When I slide my feet into my favorite slippers, immediately I think of Meghan. She has the same puffy slippers in the exact same shade of cotton candy pink. We bought them together at the mall and decided they were like friendship bracelets . . . except for our feet.

Just thinking about her makes me a weird mix of sad and mad.

Best friends are supposed to do things like buy matching friendship slippers. What they're *not* supposed to do is run against each other in class elections.

I look at my reflection in the mirror over my dresser and give myself a little pep talk.

In less than five minutes, I'm at the kitchen table with a steaming mug of microwave hot chocolate (topped with extra marshmallows), a plate of toaster waffles, a bright blue Sharpie, and a pad of paper. I nibble the edges off a waffle, then uncap the Sharpie and write **POSSIBLE CHOICES FOR VP** across the top of the pad.

After Meghan, my closest friends are the girls on my soccer team. I know I can count on them to support my campaign and help me get elected. They will be my J's. But it still leaves the question of who will be my veep.

I wash down a bite of waffle with a swig of hot chocolate.

Then I visualize the strongest players on the field. Callie Weaver, right midfielder, is known for her speed. Emily Peters, our number one forward, never gives up. And Blake Smith, striker, knows how to score and create opportunities for other players to score. I neatly write out all three names and study my list.

POSSIBLE CHOICES FOR VP

✳ Callie Weaver

✳ Emily Peters

✳ Blake Smith

The question is, who would be the best vice president? The answer is simple. Callie. She's just as fun and sweet as she is fast. She's super into soccer, but I have a feeling she'd be into class government, too. One thing is certain: I won't know until I ask.

"Penny for your thoughts," a voice says from behind me, and I jump.

"Dad! You scared me!" I grab my mug of hot chocolate to make sure it doesn't go flying off the table. "What are you doing up?"

He shoots me a curious look. "I was about to ask you the same question."

There's no denying the truth with Dad. Even if I tried, he'd get to the bottom of it faster than Meghan and I can eat through a roll of Girl Scout Thin Mints.

"Campaign troubles," I say.

Dad pulls out a chair and sits down next to me at the table. He studies me like he's trying to figure out what the issues are without me having to tell him. Dad prides himself on being a campaign clairvoyant. If there even is such a thing, I guess he's it. He motions to my mug of hot chocolate. "You know your mother would not approve of all of those marshmallows."

His voice sounds stern, but I see the twinkle in his eyes.

"Good thing Mom isn't here," I say cautiously.

Dad smiles. "The marshmallows will be our secret. How about you rustle me up a cup of that hot chocolate and tell me your campaign troubles. Let's see if we can't solve them."

I'm back at the table in no time and push the steaming mug with extra marshmallows in it toward Dad. If anyone can help, he can.

"What's going on?" he asks, getting right to the point.

I take a deep breath and the whole thing tumbles out. What happened with Meghan, Bree, the J's, and how I still don't have a vice president.

Dad slowly sips his hot chocolate, then speaks. "Amanda, years ago your mother ran for city councilwoman and one of her closest friends decided to run against her."

"Who?" I ask. I don't remember any of Mom's friends ever running against her.

Dad gives me a small smile. "You'll be surprised to hear this. It was your Aunt Julie."

"Aunt Julie?!?" I ask, shocked. She's my non-aunt aunt. My mom's friend who is more than a best friend but not family so I call her my aunt anyway.

"The very one," says Dad.

On the listening scale, my ears are a ten. "But they're still best friends. What happened?"

Dad sits back in his chair. "When Mom found out Julie was running, she wasn't happy about it. She would have preferred Julie be there to support her, not run against her. But sometimes candidates don't have a choice about who opposes them. Mom debated how to handle the situation. Finally, she decided the best thing to do was to talk to Julie."

I get what Dad is saying. That I should talk to Meghan. I tried. It didn't go well. I lean across the table toward Dad. "What did Mom say?" I ask.

"She said she planned to run a fair and upstanding campaign and hoped Julie would do the same. No mudslinging."

"You mean no saying bad things about the other candidate?"

"Exactly," Dad says. "Running a clean campaign is just as important as an effective one. And Mom and Aunt Julie agreed no matter the outcome of the election, they'd always be friends." He looks at me like he's trying to gauge if I understand what he's saying.

I do. "You mean friendship is more important than an election."

Dad nods.

I get what he's saying, but there's something he doesn't know. "I already talked to Meghan. And it didn't go well."

"If at first you don't succeed . . ."

"Try, try again," I say, finishing his sentence.

Dad nods. "And establish some ground rules."

"Like no mudslinging."

Dad gives me a thumbs-up. "That's an excellent start. Moving on to your vice president."

I push my pad of paper across the table at Dad, then tell him about all of the girls on the list. "I'm going to ask Callie." I tilt my chin up, confident in my decision. "She'd be great."

Dad clucks. It kind of makes him sound like a chicken. Except he's not one. If Dad were an animal, he'd be a dolphin or chimpanzee, the quiet but smart type.

"Amanda, I'm sure your teammates would all be excellent choices. But have you given any thought to choosing someone different from you?"

An image of Ben Ball's face flashes in front of me. No way. Not happening.

"Hear me out," says Dad like he can read my mind. "There's value in choosing a running mate who could bring something different to the table. Someone who could help you get votes from other student groups."

Other student groups! Votes! I haven't even thought about those things yet. "Um, Dad, I think you're getting a little ahead of yourself here. I need to pick a vice president first."

"All I'm saying is that you shouldn't be afraid to go with

the unexpected choice. Is there a person you can think of who might fall into that category?"

Ben's snort-laugh plays in my head like a loop. *Yep.* There's a person who falls into that category. But I'm not picking him! The way to **NOT** get elected is to have Ben Ball by my side cracking jokes that aren't funny.

"Just think about it," says Dad.

"Sure," I say. I have thought about it. And the last person I would ever pick to be my running mate is Ben Ball.

Chapter Seven

BIRDS OF A FEATHER DON'T ALWAYS FLY TOGETHER

As soon as I get to school, I hunt down Meghan. But not in a hunter-stalking-her-prey kind of way. More in the spirit of *"we need to talk."* Dad's story about Mom and Aunt Julie running against each other resonated (one of this week's vocab words) with me.

I can't stop Meghan from running against me. But I can have a real heart-to-heart with her—just the two of us—and tell her that our friendship is more important than any election and we just need some ground rules so we both run fair, clean campaigns.

Finding her is easier than I expected. There she is, standing right next to Bree Simon, on top of one of the benches in the area officially known as the seventh-grade benches. They're wearing matching bubblegum pink T-shirts that say VOTE HART AND SIMON in big raspberry-colored hearts, and just about every seventh grader I know is crowded around them.

Meghan raises a megaphone to her lips. "Free donuts!" she announces. I try to tune out the clapping and cheering as my eyes scan the crowd. That's when I see it. All of the J's are wearing the same T-shirts Meghan and Bree have on, and they're the ones giving out the donuts, which happen to have pink sprinkles on them, the same color as their T-shirts.

I focus on Meghan, using every ounce of best-friend ESP I can muster. *Look at me. Look at me!* I will her eyes to move in my direction, and it works. Her gaze meets mine, and her cheeks turn pinker than her T-shirt. She gives me a small smile, almost like she feels bad. Then she looks away, whispers something to Bree, and passes her the microphone.

"Vote Meghan Hart for class president!"

Bree's voice echoes through the crowd. She raises a donut high above her head like it's a symbol of the Hart-Simon campaign, and the crowd goes wild.

There's more clapping and cheering and it's obvious to me that sprinkle-covered donuts + cool T-shirts + Meghan and Bree for class officers = an unbeatable combo.

My plans for talking to Meghan swirl away faster than water going down a flushed toilet. I can't talk to her now. Not with every seventh grader I know (except for me and Frankie Chang, who is more like a fourth or fifth grader) chomping away on campaign-themed breakfast pastries and cheering on the Hart-Simon ticket. This campaign doesn't even officially start until next week, and already I'm sunk.

On so many levels!

This morning Dad said how important it is to run a clean campaign.

Pre-campaign donuts don't exactly fall into that category. I don't even think candidates for office are allowed to bring food to school. Plus, those T-shirts didn't just create themselves. Someone had to design and order them. And it's not like Dunkin' Donuts just happened to have one hundred pink sprinkle donuts on hand this morning.

Suddenly, it all becomes clear to me. Meghan's plans to run for class president have been in the works for a while. And she's in it to win it. Even worse, she's doing a pretty good job of it.

Until this morning, she was my best friend who was also my opponent. Now, she's what's officially known as a frontrunner. That's a word that I've heard used a lot of times in my house. It means the candidate who appears most likely to win the election, and if the cheering crowd gathered around Meghan is an indication of things to come, I'm in big trouble.

Even though I see Principal Ferguson barreling his way over to the donut giveaway like he's about to shut it down, Meghan's pre-campaign efforts have already made a **BIG** impact.

The damage has been done. "This is bad," I mumble. "Bad. Bad. Bad."

"Yep," says a voice from behind me. "It is."

I don't have to turn to know that the speaker is Ben Ball. "Adams, have you tried a donut?" He dangles one in front of my nose. The aroma is sugary sweet and delicious. But I swat it away angrily.

Ben tssks. "Now, now. Aggression never helped any candidate get elected. Don't get mad. Get even." He leans closer, then adds, "And you better hop to it. Or this campaign thing of yours will be over before it starts. Make a decision yet on a running mate?"

I open my mouth to speak. No words come out.

Ben stuffs his mouth with my opponent's donut.

- - - - - - - - - -

I shove my books into my locker and slam shut the door. The world's longest school day in the history of school days is over. *Finally!*

It was a lot of work avoiding all the people I didn't want to talk to today. Like Meghan. And Ben Ball. And Mrs. Lee. *Grrr!* I never thought my favorite teacher would be someone I wanted to avoid. She and Ben both wanted to know who I'd picked for my VP.

But I had nothing to tell them because I still don't know. Mrs. Lee even reminded me that tomorrow is the deadline. As if I could forget!

NEWS FLASH: AMANDA ADAMS IS OFFICIALLY STILL VEEPLESS!

I sprint from my locker to the gym. All I want to do is to put on my soccer cleats and get out on the field with my team. Today, I have a lot on my mind besides blocking goals.

When I get to the field, Callie Weaver is already there. She's always one of the first to arrive, because she's the fastest one on our team, and because she has last-period gym, which means she's already right where she needs to be for practice. She's running her warm-up laps around the field and I fall into place beside her.

"Hey, girl!" She grins cheerily at me.

I smile, for what feels like the first time all day. Callie is my number one pick for vice president. She's strong and smart, fast and funny, and best of all, sweet. She'd make a great class officer. I take a deep breath, filling my lungs with air and hope.

"So, there's something I want to talk to you about," I say. "Don't know if you've heard, but I'm running for president of our class."

Her grin disappears. "Mmm hmm," she mumbles.

On the excitement scale, Callie's *mmm-hmm* was a two. My stomach knots, but I do my best to ignore the feeling and continue.

"So, I need a vice president." I glance at her. "Job is yours if you want it. And I really hope you do, because you'd make a great VP. Interested?"

Callie doesn't answer my question. Instead, she picks up her pace.

Keeping up with her is hard. Keeping up with her while trying to have a serious conversation is even harder. The field is starting to fill up with other team members, and Callie runs over to a group of seventh-grade players that includes Emily Peters, Blake Smith, and Zoey Thompson. "Meeting," she calls, and everyone huddles around her. Her mouth opens to speak, and instinct tells me I'm not going to like what she has to say.

"I'm pretty sure everyone has already heard: Amanda is running for president of our class."

I try to look NOT WORRIED while my teammates all look at me.

"Yeah!" I say cheerily. "I was just asking Callie if she wants to be my vice president. And I really want all of you to help me on my campaign." I flash them a big smile. "How cool would it be if our team was in control of things like planning the class dance and the community service project? Right?"

Everyone just blinks. It's pretty obvious they don't think it sounds nearly as cool as I do.

I keep talking. "This election is really important to me, and I need your support."

I close my mouth, waiting for someone, anyone, to say I have it. But Emily looks at Blake, who looks at Zoey, then all eyes settle on Callie like she's the designated spokesperson.

Callie clears her throat. "Amanda, we were going to talk to you about this whole election thing. We don't think it's a good idea for you to run. I mean, you're our goalie. It's kind of a big deal that Coach Newton put you in such an important position. We need you to win games," says Callie. "And the game against Brookside is next week."

"I know," I say. Everyone knows how important it is to beat our biggest rival.

"So, how are you going to have time to run a campaign and then a whole class *and* play soccer, too?" asks Callie.

I try to imitate Mom's TV smile. "Lots of kids do more than one thing at school."

"True," says Zoey.

I exhale, relieved that at least someone is being reasonable. But my relief is short-lived.

"Thing is," says Blake, "we're worried you'll be spending all of your time making campaign posters and writing speeches."

I shake my head. "Not when I'm supposed to be at practice."

My teammates exchange a look that says this is something they've talked about. "You really think it's a good idea to run for class president?" asks Emily. "Because we don't."

I hold up my right arm like I'm taking a courtroom oath

to tell the truth. "Winning games is just as important to me as winning this election. Running for class president won't interfere with playing on our soccer team. I promise."

"Our *winning* soccer team," corrects Zoey. "Don't forget Brookside has beaten us three straight years. We have to break the streak."

"I know. I know." Anyone even remotely interested in girls' soccer at Liberty Middle School knows that our archrival has smoked our you-know-whats for the last three years. And that Coach Newton is determined this year's game will be our redemption.

I get that winning is important. Especially against Brookside. And I get that Coach Newton and my team are trusting me to do a great job as goalie. I want to win games just as much as they do. But I also want to be president of my class.

And to run, I need a veep. Callie doesn't want the job. And beggars can't be choosy. "So does anyone here want to be my running mate?" I wait for someone . . . ANYONE . . . to say they do. But no one does.

Coach Newton blows her whistle. It's time for practice to begin. My teammates disperse (a vocab word that I wish I wasn't using) and head out to the field. Me being president of my class might not be what my lifelong best friend or my teammates want, but it's what I want.

Now, I just have to figure out how to make it happen.

***

MY CAMPAIGN INSPIRATION NOTEBOOK

✸ Abraham Lincoln ✸

BORN: February 12, 1809, Hardin County, Kentucky

DIED: April 14, 1865. Assassinated at Ford's Theatre in Washington, D.C., by John Wilkes Booth

SIGN: Aquarius. Traits: Charming, impulsive, romantic, nonconformist.

PARTY: Republican

STATUS: Married to Mary Todd Lincoln

KIDS: Four boys. Robert, Edward, William, Thomas

PRESIDENCY: He became the 16th president of our nation in 1861.

NICKNAME: Honest Abe

PETS: Horses, turkeys, rabbits, goats, cats, AND DOGS! (That man loved animals, almost as much as he loved the idea of equality for all.)

HEIGHT: 6 feet 4 inches (he was the tallest president), and with his stovepipe hat on (and he never took it off) he was almost 7 feet tall! Legend has it that he stored things like letters and documents in his hat.

SIDE GIG: Story and joke teller

FAMOUS SPEECH: The Gettysburg Address

PRESIDENTIAL CHALLENGE: A nation divided!!!

Interest in my inspiration notebook has gone from a 1 (when Dad first suggested the idea) to a 9.5 (now that it's evident I need all the help I can get).

And what president could be more inspiring than Good Ole Abe. I mean, half of a country was against him and he still got the job done. Surely he can provide some much-needed inspiration, because I truly, madly, desperately need some.

Okay. Here goes.

One: Growing up, Abe didn't have it easy.

He was born in a one-room log cabin, and his family struggled to get by. When he was nine, his mother died and his older sister took care of him. Abe had little formal education, but a strong interest in books and learning. In fact, most of what he learned was from books he read on his own. As a young man, Lincoln worked as a shopkeeper, surveyor, and postmaster. He even split firewood for a living. All before going into politics!

Bottom line: If you want to be president, become a surveyor first.

Ha! I don't think a career reading maps or checking out land would help me get elected class president. I guess the lesson here is that the journey to political success isn't always easy.

(Note to self: REMEMBER THAT!)

Two: Even though Abe had it tough growing up, being president was even tougher.

Seriously, he had a very tough job as our president because

when he was elected, a bunch of states in the South didn't want him to be president. They didn't like his policies on slavery, so what did they do? They up and left the country and formed a new one called the Confederacy. Bad, huh? It gets worse. Just a month after he took office, the Civil War started and it lasted four long years and claimed hundreds of thousands of American lives.

During that time, Lincoln faced all kinds of opposition, but he persisted and managed to free the slaves and hold the country together. It wasn't easy. He even advocated (another well-used vocab word!) forgiveness for the South and helped the states that had seceded from the nation to heal and rebuild. Then, after all of that, he was assassinated.

> **Bottom line: Becoming a leader and then being one isn't always easy. But you can't give up. That's the lesson here. Just because two sides want different things doesn't mean a leader should quit. No way! A true leader doesn't quit. A true leader finds a way to make it happen.**

Seriously! If Abe Lincoln could figure out how to deal with half a nation going against him, I can find a way to deal with a best friend gone rogue and a few disgruntled teammates.

Oh yeah, and find a vice president by tomorrow.

Pas de problème. That's French for I CAN DO THIS THING!

Chapter Eight
TICK TOCK

I t takes effort, but I don't slam Dad's car door as I get out. Even though I want to. Being greeted by none other than Ben Ball was not how I planned to start my school day.

He grins at me. "Word on the street is that you're still veepless."

I sling my backpack over one shoulder and begin the walk toward homeroom. Right now, I have one purpose and one purpose only: to ask Annalise Robey (who sits in the desk behind me in homeroom and starts every day by offering me a Pep-O-Mint Life Savers) if she wants to be my vice president.

I thought about it a lot last night, and Annalise is definitely my best option.

She's popular, but not so popular that she would make less

popular people feel bad. Pretty, but not so pretty that other girls would hate her for it. Smart, but not so smart that less industrious students might feel inferior. And she always smells minty fresh.

She also happens to be a piano virtuoso. Not a required skill for a running mate, but a good one. Who knows, maybe Annalise can come up with some original theme music for our campaign. A Jonas Brothers melody pops into my head.

"Umm . . . Adams . . . did you hear me?"

I walk, head down, pretending I didn't hear Ben. It's a hint that he doesn't pick up on. He falls into step beside me. "Adams, did I hear it right? You're still veepless?"

I clear my throat. "Veepless isn't a word."

Ben cackles. "It will be if you don't find someone soon to be your running mate. I heard that no one on the soccer team wants you to run."

I come to an immediate halt. My mouth falls open. "How did you hear that?"

Ben taps both sides of his head. "Adams, didn't ya know I have 20/20 hearing?"

I smirk. "Don't you mean vision?"

Ben waves a hand through the air. "That too. Point is, I make it my business to know what's going on around Liberty Middle. And what I know is that if you don't act fast, you're going to be out of the race." On the loudness scale, his voice is a seven. Other kids are looking our way as Ben keeps talking. "The incomparable Miss Meghan H. and Baby Bree . . ."

I motion for him to keep his voice down. "Please don't call them that."

"Duly noted," Ben says. He starts talking again, but this time (thankfully) his voice is a little lower. "Word on the street is that the football team is planning to vote for Meghan and Bree." He shrugs. "What can I say? Athletes like donuts. And Frankie Chang already has the honor society on lockdown. I think he promised them all that if they vote for him, his father will teach them how to build a robot that can make their bed."

"A robot can do that?" I ask.

"Appealing, isn't it?" asks Ben. "But not what we need to be discussing." He pulls a sheet of paper from his back pocket and starts to read from it.

LIBERTY MIDDLE SCHOOL

CLASS PRESIDENT

The president of each middle school grade will preside over class government meetings and be the liaison between the school administration and parent boosters. In addition, the class president will be directly responsible for leading all efforts to plan the class dance and community service project.

The class president may also represent the school at functions outside of school, such as school board meetings or in the community. Class president is a challenging position that offers an excellent opportunity for building communication and leadership skills.

CLASS VICE PRESIDENT

The vice president is responsible for supporting the president in all student government activities. In addition, the vice president will take over duties of the president if she or he is unable or must resign due to a move or a change of school. This also means the vice president may oversee meetings or functions if the president is out of town or absent due to illness. In addition, the vice president will help recruit volunteers and delegate responsibilities to volunteer committees.

When Ben finishes reading the job descriptions of class president and vice president, he refolds the paper and slips it back into his pocket. I shoot him a tell-me-something-I-don't-know look. I've read those descriptions so many times that I've practically got them memorized.

"Okay. I'll bottom line it," says Ben. "You need to pick me for your vice president. For a couple of reasons. One, I have an engaging personality."

I clamp my lips shut. I'm not sure *engaging* is how I would describe it.

Ben continues. "Two, aside from being a comic genius, I'm also a brilliant political strategist."

An image of my dad pops into my mind. Not sure he and Ben fall into the same category.

"What do you know about running a campaign?" I ask, immediately regretting the question. What's the point of hearing Ben's answer when I'm planning to ask Annalise to be my running mate?

Ben doesn't bother answering anyway.

"Adams, there's a third reason you need to pick me." He pauses, like he's waiting for a drumroll. "If you don't have a veep by end of day today, you're out of the race."

He's not wrong about that. Mrs. Lee is expecting me to give her the name of my running mate by the end of the day. My eyes scan the seventh-grade benches for Annalise.

"So," says Ben.

"I appreciate that you want the job, but I was planning to offer it to Annalise Robey."

No sooner is her name out of my mouth than Ben starts snort-laughing so loud that I'm pretty sure kids who go to middle schools in neighboring states like Maryland and West Virginia (and even as far away as Kentucky and Tennessee) can hear him. "Life Savers girl?"

The way Ben asks the question makes me defensive on her part. "Yeah," I say, my hands now on my hips. "I think she'd make a great veep. And what's wrong with good breath?"

The corners of Ben's mouth curl up. "If you think she'd be so good, ask her. Hey, Annalise," he calls out over my shoulder, and just like that Annalise materializes beside me. "Amanda has a question for you. Go on," he says to me. "Ask her."

I brush a stray curl off of my face. This wasn't how I wanted to ask, but now it's not like I have another choice. "Umm, Annalise, don't know if you heard, but I'm running for president of our class." I flash a smile that I hope conveys both confidence and friendliness. "I wanted to know if you'd like to run with me, as my vice president?"

"Thank you," says Annalise.

On the enthusiasm scale, she's a three. I press my lips together and shift nervously from one foot to the other while I wait for her to elaborate.

Annalise blows out a breath and I smell mint. "I have a big piano recital coming up," she says. "All my free time is spent practicing. And my mom would never let me take time off from practicing to run." Annalise shoots me a look like she's embarrassed to have such a strict parent. "I'm sorry, Amanda. See you in homeroom."

"Sure," I say.

Ben hardly waits for Annalise to walk off. "So, Adams, why not pick me? Admit it. You know I'd do a great job. Plus, it seems I'm the only person who wants it."

I scratch a mosquito bite on my left wrist. It's kind of impressive that Ben had the job descriptions in his back pocket. And that he wants to do it.

The first bell rings. Ben's eyes narrow at me. "You have exactly ten seconds before this offer expires. Tick tock, Adams. Tick tock."

I picture Mrs. Lee's face and what it will look like if I tell her that Ben Ball is my running mate. He drives teachers crazy, even crazier than he drives his fellow students. My favorite teacher will be surprised. Shocked. Definitely concerned that I've lost my mind.

Zut alors! In French, that means I want to tear out my hair.

"Okay," I say.

Ben squeals louder than Meghan and I do when we've come across a bargain at the mall. He looks so happy that I think he's going to hug me. I take a step back to make sure he doesn't.

"Adams, you won't regret this," he says.

Something tells me I already do.

LIBERTY MIDDLE SCHOOL

FROM: THE OFFICE OF PRINCIPAL FERGUSON
TO: ALL CANDIDATES RUNNING FOR CLASS OFFICERS

Student Candidates:
Congratulations on your decision to run for the position of class president/vice president. Following is an explanation of the rules and guidelines that will govern this campaign as well as the schedule of events. Please read this document carefully, and return the form, signed by you and a parent, to my office on Monday morning.

Good luck to you all,
Principal Ferguson

CAMPAIGN RULES/SCHEDULE
& ELECTION GUIDELINES

Campaigns will take place from Tuesday, October 1, to Thursday, October 10. During this time, candidates may hang no more than six posters in the Liberty Middle School hallways and cafeteria. Posters must be appropriate for school and may not harm anyone else involved in the running for office. Stickers and/or buttons promoting your candidacy may also be distributed.

A word of caution: Use common sense when creating campaign materials. If you aren't sure what is appropriate, ask Mrs. Lee. Anything inappropriate will be taken down, and you could risk losing your candidacy.

DISTRIBUTION OF CANDY OR OTHER FOOD ITEMS ON SCHOOL PREMISES IS STRICTLY PROHIBITED.

Interviews of all presidential candidates will be conducted on our campus TV station on Tuesday, October 8, and broadcast live to grade-level homerooms.

Final campaign speeches will be conducted on Thursday, October 10. Each presidential candidate is expected to give a speech up to three minutes in length. All speeches must be turned in to Mrs. Lee for approval no later than first period, Wednesday, October 9. Following the speeches, ballots will be distributed. Election results will be tallied and announced by end of school on Thursday, October 10.

All candidates must pledge to maintain the highest standards of personal conduct, to act in the best interests of their school, to reflect opinions of the students they represent to the best of their ability, to promote school spirit, and to practice effective leadership and good citizenship.

I understand the requirements and duties of the office I am applying for and agree to commit to the campaign rules as outlined above.

Student signature: *Amanda Adams*

Parent signature: *Congresswoman Carol Adams*

Chapter Nine

TWO NOSES (PLUS AN ADDITIONAL TWO) TO ONE GRINDSTONE

(AND YOUR SECRETS ARE SAFE WITH ME)

I prop my elbows on my kitchen table, and my chin sinks into my hands. It's pretty hard not to think about the fact that it's Saturday, and instead of the sleepover I have every weekend with Meghan, I'm sitting here, at the kitchen table, working on my campaign with Ben.

"Adams, we need to think big," says Ben. "BIG! BIG! BIG!"

He's right. We do need to think **BIG.** Especially after Meghan's breakfast giveaway. *Le petit dejeuner.* That's what you call breakfast in French. Not that it matters.

I push Principal Ferguson's letter across the table at Ben and jab my finger at the line about distribution of food. "Meghan is lucky she gave out those donuts before Principal Ferguson gave all of the candidates this letter saying she couldn't."

Ben waves a hand through the air. "One preemptive strike won't kill us."

He's right. Dad would say, *"You can't change the past, so focus on the future."* Which is what I intend to do.

I clear my throat. "Step one to winning an election is getting our names out there," I say. Then I remind Ben that posters can go up, and we can start handing out stickers on Tuesday. "That means we need to get everything finished this weekend so we'll be ready to put up the posters and pass out the stickers first thing Tuesday morning."

"Agreed." Ben nods.

"So," I continue, "I have an idea for a slogan." But before I tell it to Ben, I show him my inspiration notebook and tell him my parents are making me keep it. I wait for him to snort-laugh so loud that Mom and Dad (and the Cooper family that lives next door) will all come running to our kitchen to see what's so funny.

But to his credit, Ben doesn't snort-laugh. "That's cool," he says, flipping through the pages. When he gets to the one about Thomas Jefferson, I stop him. Then I tell him my idea.

"TJ's face is on every nickel out there. What if we make stickers and posters with nickels on them, but instead of TJ's face, we put ours on them with the campaign slogan "Face It, Adams and Ball Are the Best Choices for Seventh Grade President and Vice President."

Ben purses his lips.

"Or not," I say, suddenly self-conscious that my idea might not be such a good one.

A slow smile spreads over Ben's face. "Adams, you're a campaign genius. That's brilliant," Ben says. "I love it!"

"So do we," say a duo of voices accompanied by a chorus of clapping.

I turn slowly in my chair to face my parents, who have somehow materialized in the kitchen. No telling how long they'd been hiding behind the door, waiting for the right moment to make their presence known. "Mom, Dad, I got this. Really," I say.

I made it very clear before Ben showed up this morning that this was *my* campaign. Not theirs. And when he arrived, I made all of the introductions and told Mom and Dad that Ben and I would be working in the kitchen. It was a hint (which *clearly* they didn't get) that they could choose any room in our house to hang out in. EXCEPT THE KITCHEN!

"Oh, Amanda." Mom says my name like I'm being silly. "We want to support you."

"The more noses to the grindstone, the better," adds Dad. He goes into the pantry and returns with a bag of Oreos and offers it to Ben. "Ben, you like cookies, don't you?"

"Love them." Ben helps himself to a big handful.

Mom gives him an approving smile, and that's all it takes. "Honestly, Amanda, no one knows more about campaigns than your parents," Ben says. "It can't hurt to get their input."

"We'd love to help in any way we can," says Dad.

"We really would," adds Mom.

Three sets of eyeballs shift in my direction like they're all waiting for me to grant permission for two campaign pros to help two novices. "Fine," I mumble.

My parents exhale like they just scored front row seats to a Taylor Swift concert.

I twist off the top of an Oreo and stuff it into my mouth. For the next half hour, Ben, my parents, and I eat Oreos and talk about slogans. Ours shifts from putting our faces on a nickel to putting them on a hundred-dollar bill with the slogan: "Vote Adams and Ball, the Most Valuable Candidates for Seventh Grade President and Vice President."

Once that's decided, we make a list of all the supplies we need to make stickers and posters, and Dad volunteers to drive us to Target to get what we need.

"Adams, we're off to the races," says Ben as we get into Dad's car. We high-five. And I have to admit, I'm feeling better than I have all week about our campaign.

- - - - - - - - - -

Dad peels off a neat stack of bills from the wad of cash in his wallet. He gives me the cash, then says he'll wait in the car while Ben and I get what we need at Target. We make our way through the weekend crowds shopping for clothes, home goods, and food, and head straight to the art supplies aisle.

But before we get there, I hear a laugh I know better than my own.

"Ben!" I hiss his name, then pull him down the party supplies aisle and use his body like a shield to protect me from the unmistakable sounds of a certain someone's laughter that is getting closer . . . and closer . . . and closer!

Ben pivots, then places a hand on my forehead like he's checking to see if I've developed a sudden fever. "Adams, what the heck is the matter?" he asks.

But before I answer, I'm face-to-face with Meghan, Bree, and the J's. Meghan and I are wearing the same shirts. The Hello Kitty ones we bought on sale at the end of sixth grade.

"Ladies," says Ben, breaking the silence. "You look armed and ready."

Dangerous. I think that's the word he should have used.

"Hi, Amanda," stammers Meghan. "We were just picking up a few art supplies."

Even though Meghan and I have been best friends for a long time, our definition of *a few* is clearly different. "Looks like a lot," I say, eyeballing what they're carrying: a thick stack of pink poster boards, boxes of markers, jars of paint, an assortment of brushes, glue sticks, tubes of glitter, rolls of ribbon, pink felt, pink streamers, and bags of confetti. My mind reels. What are they going to do with confetti? This is an election. Not a New Year's Eve party.

Meghan opens her mouth to say something, but Bree beats her to it.

"We better get going," she says.

"Yeah. See ya around," adds Meghan.

"See you around," I say. Meghan and her crew go one way, and Ben and I the other. But as they walk off, the skin on my neck feels prickly hot.

"Um, that was awkward," I whisper as soon as the sound of their footsteps has faded away. I fight off an unexpected urge to cry.

"Adams, you okay?" Ben asks as we make our way to the art supplies.

Even though Ben Ball is the last person I would ever consider confiding in, he is my running mate. And the only person around for me to talk to. And right now, I'm a ten on the need-to-talk-to-someone scale. I stop in front of the display of poster boards and study it.

What color should we buy? *White or green?* I can't decide and pull out some of both. "Truth?" I finally ask.

"Your secrets are safe with me," says Ben.

My eyes search his, unsure if I can trust a kid who up until this week I hardly knew. Not to mention he's also known as the class clown. Do I want to spill my guts to him and end up the butt of some bad joke? On the other hand . . . well . . . I don't even know what the other hand might be. "Seriously, Ben, if you tell anybody what I'm about to say, I'll kill you."

He laughs. "Adams, in case you haven't heard, murderers don't get elected president. Hey, what's it called if you kill your friend?" Ben doesn't wait before delivering the punch line. "Homie-cide."

I can't help but smile. Then I blow out a breath and start talking. "I'm pretty upset about the whole way this went down with Meghan." I pause, taking a moment to choose my words carefully. "It just sucks that she went behind my back the way she did."

"Yeah," says Ben. "It does. Not very best-friend-ly."

Having someone else see what I see feels good.

"Did you see all that stuff they were buying?" I ask Ben.

"Couldn't miss it," he says, then mumbles something about fighting fire with fire, or in this case, art supplies. He grabs a pack of green construction paper. "Maybe we should buy this to make the hundred-dollar bills."

"Good idea," I say, grabbing a pack of black Sharpies. *And* some labels we can use as stickers. *And* some green and black paint and brushes. *And* a box of colored markers. Then I give

Ben a long, hard look. "I'm afraid we have a **LOT** of work to do if we're going to win this election."

"Adams," he says, "I'm afraid you're right."

✳ ✳ ✳

MY CAMPAIGN INSPIRATION NOTEBOOK

THEODORE AND FRANKLIN ROOSEVELT, AKA THE R'S (LIKE THE J'S EXCEPT TOTALLY DIFFERENT)

✳ Theodore Roosevelt ✳

BORN: October 27, 1858, New York, NY
DIED: January 6, 1919, New York
SIGN: Scorpio. Traits: Passionate, ambitious.
PARTY: Republican
STATUS: Married
KIDS: Five of them
NICKNAMES: Teddy (which he hated) and TR (the first president to be known by his initials)
PETS: TR loved animals, especially dogs. He had lots of them. And he let his kids have lots of pets, too, including a lizard, a pig, a badger, a rooster, an owl, and a small bear.
SIDE HUSTLE: Writer. He wrote 35 books and 15,000 letters.
FAMOUS SPEECH: "The Man in the Arena"

✳ Franklin Delano Roosevelt ✳

BORN: January 30, 1882, Hyde Park, NY
DIED: April 12, 1945, in Georgia
SIGN: Aquarius. Traits: Wit and imagination.
PARTY: Democrat
STATUS: Married to Eleanor Roosevelt
KIDS: Six of them
NICKNAMES: FDR
PETS: Lots of dogs, including Fala and Meggie, both Scottish terriers; Major, a German shepherd; President, a Great Dane; and Tiny, an Old English Sheepdog.
HOBBIES: Boating and stamp collecting (he had over a million stamps!)
FAMOUS SPEECH: The "Infamy" speech

✳ ✳ ✳

Ben and I did a lot of work this weekend. Our posters are really good. So are our stickers. Come Tuesday, we're putting it all out there for everyone to see and judge for themselves.

And that makes me a little nervous. Okay, a lot nervous.

It just feels like we have some obstacles to face if we want to win this election.

Like running against Meghan. And Bree. And knowing they have Jayda, the best artist in our grade, on their side.

When I asked Mom which president I should look at who faced lots of obstacles, she suggested President Roosevelt. Well, there were two of them, and I'm not sure which one she meant. So I'm looking at them both—Theodore Roosevelt, our nation's twenty-sixth president, and Franklin Delano Roosevelt, our thirty-second president—to see what these fifth cousins really do know about obstacles.

First, Theodore Roosevelt.

TR believed that the success of democracy was about three things: hard work, character, and having a leader who set an example for others. He was a strong president. (I don't know how much weight he could lift.) TR was known for his passion (There is something to this zodiac stuff!) and for getting crowds going with his loud voice and fist pounding. He worked long and hard on matters that were important to him, like conservation and world peace. He even won a Nobel Prize for his efforts.

But he faced some pretty big obstacles, too.

> *Obstacle #1: Before he ever became president, his first wife and his mother died on the same day. He spent two years in the Badlands of the Dakota Territory driving cattle and grieving.*
>
> **Bottom line: I don't know much about cattle driving, but I kind of get the grief thing. Losing your best friend isn't the same thing as losing someone who dies. But still it hurts.**

Maybe in time Meghan and I will be friends again. *Or not???*

> *Obstacle #2: Republican leaders didn't want Roosevelt to be president. They didn't like some of his policies, or the way he went about things. But he kept going anyway . . . all the way to the Oval Office.*

Bottom line: I have to keep going all the way to the office of seventh-grade class president despite any obstacles.

Obstacle #3: While in the White House, TR went blind in one eye after a boxing injury. His retina detached and he had to stop fighting, so he took up jujitsu instead.

Bottom line: I'm sticking with soccer.

TR liked to hunt, and in 1902 he got invited on a bear hunt by the governor of Mississippi. When TR hadn't found a single bear, one of the governor's assistants cornered a bear and tied it to a tree for the president to shoot. TR thought it was unsportsmanlike and refused to do it. News spread fast that he refused to shoot a bear. There was even a political cartoon making fun of him. But TR didn't mind. He even laughed about it. Then a toy company started making stuffed bears and called them Teddy bears!

Good to know that TR had a sense of humor even when he faced obstacles.

Now, on to Frankie D.

One of the things he's most famous for is the "Infamy" speech. FDR delivered it to a joint session of Congress on December 8, 1941, the day after Japan attacked Pearl Harbor, Hawaii, and unexpectedly declared war on the United States. Going to war was a **HUGE** obstacle he faced. More on that later, because war wasn't his only obstacle.

Obstacle #1: In the summer of 1921, when FDR was only thirty-nine years old, he came down with polio, a disease that left him paralyzed from the waist down and unable to walk. Despite this, he went on to become governor of New York and was elected President of the United States FOUR times! That's more than any other president.

Bottom line: Never give up!

Obstacle #2: When FDR was elected president in 1932, the United States was in the depths of the Great Depression. Thirteen million people were unemployed, and almost every bank in the nation was closed. Despite tremendous challenges, he helped revitalize (not a vocab word, but sounds like it should be) the economy and got the American people believing in themselves again. He told them: The only thing we have to fear is fear itself.

Bottom line: Even when things seem scary, the only thing to be scared of is being scared.

Obstacle #3: World War II!

For many years, FDR tried to prevent the involvement of United States troops in the war. He helped many countries in Europe through his policies and aid, but when the Japanese attacked Pearl Harbor, Roosevelt declared war against Japan, and the United States took military action. FDR refused to let up until the Japanese and the Nazi regime were defeated. FDR knew that when the war ended, the future of world peace would be at stake, so he worked hard in his later years to find ways to ease international tensions. But his health worsened. On

April 12, 1945, he died while in
Georgia, of a brain hemorrhage.

Bottom line: Being a leader means fighting until
the end for what you believe in.

Bottom, bottom line: The R's faced lots of
obstacles, but they kept on keeping on.

And so will I!

Chapter Ten
NOT ALL PRINCIPALS LIKE BREAKFAST BURRITOS

Dad pulls into the morning drop-off line and brakes before he's supposed to. The driver of the car behind us honks like crazy. But it does nothing to get Dad to move forward.

"Amanda, why is a food truck that sells burritos parked in front of your school with your name plastered all over it?" he asks.

Holy guacamole!

That's actually one of the specialties the food truck in question sells.

"Don't know," I say. I then hop out of the car before Mom or Dad has a chance to ask me any more about it.

My eyes scan the scene. There's a Bob's Burritos truck with a huge sign on the side of it that says: VOTE ADAMS AND BALL. And there beside it is Ben. Smiling. Handing out sheets of paper to every seventh grader in sight. By the sea of smiles and head nods, it looks like whatever is on that paper is making the people who are getting it pretty freaking happy.

I rush over to the scene. "Ben, what's going on?!?" I whisper, careful to keep my voice at a two on the loudness scale. Attracting any more attention than the looks I'm already getting is NOT my goal. Ben shoves a stack of papers into my hands and I look down at them.

"Adams, kids like donuts. But they *LOVE* breakfast burritos."

"BEN!" I hiss. "Remember what Principal Ferguson said about giving out food?"

Ben shoots me a sly smile. "I'm not giving out food. I'm giving out coupons for food. Subtle but important difference," he adds.

My mouth falls open, but before any words come out of it, Ben keeps talking.

"I've worked for my Uncle Bob every Saturday for two years for free. He owes me one, and now I'm cashing in my chips. For burritos." He adds, "All is fair in love or war."

I see Meghan and Bree at the edge of the crowd. Meghan's eyes meet mine and I look away. "This isn't love or war," I shoot back at Ben. "It's a campaign."

"Yes," he responds. "And if it's one you want to win, you have to think **BIG**."

I glance at the Bob's Burritos truck behind me. It isn't big. It's **ENORMOUS!**

Then I see Principal Ferguson marching toward the food truck. He doesn't look like a man who has fluffy eggs wrapped in warm tortillas on his mind.

"Better to ask forgiveness than permission," Ben mumbles under his breath.

Only, I'm not so sure about that. Principal Ferguson is a big guy. Not food truck big. But not far off. His eyes flash with a fury that makes him look like an angry bear.

"Adams, Ball, in my office immediately!" he barks.

What happens next is a blur. The kids surrounding the food truck are sent to their homerooms. Uncle Bob is told to move his food truck—away from the school. Then Ben, Meghan, Bree, Frankie Chang, Annalise Robey, and I all end up in Principal Ferguson's office waiting for him to show. My head is spinning with LOTS and LOTS of questions.

My first one is for Annalise. "What are you doing here?" I ask, unsure what she has in common with the rest of the group.

Annalise shifts from one foot to the other. "When I told my mom that you asked me to run with you, she said it would be good for me. But you'd already picked Ben, so I asked Frankie if he was looking for a veep. And he was."

I frown. "I thought you said your mom would never let you run."

Annalise shrugs. "I was wrong."

My attention shifts to Ben. The rest of my questions are for him. But I can't ask them out loud. What was he thinking, bringing a food truck to school with our names all over it? And why didn't he tell me about it before he did it? I mean seriously! It's *our* campaign. Not just *his*. And because of what he did, we're all sitting in the principal's office.

"Just trying to help the cause," Ben says, like he can read my mind.

Meghan and Bree shoot each other a look I can't quite interpret. Probably they are thinking that with Ben's help they'll win the election *sans problèmes*. That's French for winning this election will be a piece of cake. Or, in their case, a few pink sprinkle-covered donuts.

Principal Ferguson storms into his office, sits down behind his desk, and glares at the six of us. He's wearing a blue tie with red rulers and yellow pencils on it. I glance at Meghan. His school-themed ties are something we both find hilarious.

Our eyes meet instantly and we both press our lips shut so neither of us bursts out laughing. For a split second it's like we're still best friends and not opponents; then Principal Ferguson starts talking. Bree pokes Meghan and the moment is gone.

"You were all given the rules that govern this election. One of those rules was that no food may be distributed as part of the campaign."

Frankie and Annalise are busy writing down every word Principal Ferguson says, even though neither has broken that rule (and don't seem the type who would break any rule).

Meghan shifts uncomfortably in her chair, and Bree's lips curl up into a smug smile.

Ben raises his hand and speaks before Principal Ferguson calls on him. "To be clear, no food was distributed. Only coupons for food." He points a finger at Meghan and Bree. "Unlike their campaign, which distributed over ten dozen donuts last week."

"Eight," corrects Bree.

Meghan elbows her in the ribs. It's a shush elbow, and I've felt it in my rib cage more times than I can count. "We gave out donuts before we got the rule sheet," Meghan says. "Bree and I promise not to do it again. We wouldn't have done it the first time if we'd known it wasn't allowed."

"And now that we know food trucks and coupons to be redeemed at food trucks aren't allowed either, Amanda and I promise the same," says Ben.

The bell signaling students to go to their first period sounds, and Principal Ferguson's face turns redder than the rulers on his tie. "Students, I expect each one of you to follow the rules of this election. One more infraction and you're disqualified. Understand?"

We all acknowledge that we do, and Principal Ferguson sends us to our first-period classes. Everyone hurries out of his office, but I hang back and wait for Ben. There's something I need to say to him *maintenant*. In French, that means right this very second!

"Ben," I say as we walk down the hallway.

He holds up a hand, traffic-cop style. "I'm sorry, Adams. I really am. I should have asked you about the food truck before I did it."

"Yeah," I say, somewhat disarmed by his quick apology.

"After what happened at Target, I . . ." Ben stops talking, like he's suddenly not sure how to finish his sentence. When he starts again, his voice is uncharacteristically soft. "Truth is, I felt bad about the whole Meghan thing, and I wanted to do something nice for you."

Huh? Is this class clown Ben Ball talking?

"You probably didn't peg me as the *nice* type," Ben says. "But I have my moments."

"Seriously, thanks," I say, touched by his gesture.

Then I continue. "But we're *on the same ticket.*" That's a phrase Mom and Dad use with the same frequency most parents say *"brush your teeth"* or *"drink your milk,"* and I need to be sure Ben understands what it means.

"We're a team," I say. "That means making all decisions together."

"You're right," says Ben. "But you've got to admit the burritos were a nice touch."

My stomach rumbles at the idea of warm eggs, cheese, and salsa. "Not bad," I admit.

Ben grins, then raises his hand oath-style and vows that from here on out we'll work as a team. He adds, "But what's good for the goose is good for the gander. Get it, Adams?"

I roll my eyes. I'm not the one who didn't work as a team, but I raise my hand anyway and vow to do so. Then I remind Ben that tomorrow morning we can put up the posters and start handing out the stickers we spent all weekend making.

"Let's meet outside the cafeteria early so we can get a head start on Meghan and Frankie," I suggest.

"Adams and Ball. In it to win it," Ben says so loudly that a few of the kids still straggling into their first-period classes turn to look in our direction.

He raises a militant fist into the air, and I'm filled with a surge of hope.

"Adams and Ball. In it to win it!" I say as I round the corner to Mr. Corbett's classroom.

For the first time, I feel like a team with Ben. We worked hard all weekend on our campaign materials. I know Meghan and Bree worked hard as well, and I'm sure Frankie and Annalise did, too, but I can't wait to show the rest of my grade who Ben and I are as candidates.

This time tomorrow, we'll be doing just that.

Chapter Eleven
WANNABES AND GONNABES

The sun is barely up. The parking lot is still empty. There's not a school bus in sight, yet Ben and I are here, ready to unleash our campaign on Liberty Middle School. Or, at least on the seventh grade. "Thanks, Dad," I say as Ben and I gather up our supplies.

"The early bird gets the worm," Dad says (for the fourth time since we picked up Ben). Then he gives each of us fist bumps as we get out of the backseat of his car.

"Ben, let's do this," I say, my heart beating faster (maybe from excitement, nerves, or both). When I walk inside the school doors, my fingers tighten around the roll of masking tape in my hand, and I stare at the giant pink arrow pointing in the direction of the cafeteria. I don't know what it's pointing to, but instinctively I know I'm not going to like it.

"Um, why do I feel like this is bad?" I mumble to Ben, who is carrying our posters.

"Now, now," he says. "Keep walking."

We move toward the cafeteria, the hub of life at Liberty Middle School, and the place where Ben and I are planning to put up two of our six posters.

On the way, we pass Al Reed and Zavier Spencer, two candidates for eighth-grade class officers who also happen to be the best players on the basketball team and shoo-ins to win their class election. They're putting up their posters outside the science lab.

When he sees us, Zavier grins, then flashes us an "L" sign with his hand.

"Ignore him," instructs Ben.

We pass two of the sixth-grade candidates hanging their posters by the band room. But when we get to the cafeteria, my jaw falls. There, outside the entrance to the cafeteria, are Meghan, Bree, and the J's hanging all six of their hot pink posters cut into the shape of one big heart. Written in huge glitter letters are the words VOTE HART AND SIMON FOR THE SEVENTH GRADE.

Ben breathes out one word. "Wow!"

Wow is right. Their posters are one giant billboard for their campaign, and the effect is dazzling. Not a word I've ever used, but there's no other word that fits. Their poster is so good that if I weren't running against Meghan and Bree, I'd vote for them. If I had to compare our six small, hundred-dollar-bill posters with the one big heart poster Meghan and Bree put up, I'd give ours a zero on the effectiveness scale and theirs a ten (or higher).

"I bet our stickers are better," Ben mumbles.

Something tells me they're not. FDR's famous words roll around in my brain: *The only thing we have to fear is fear itself.* He faced a lot of big obstacles—disease, the Great Depression, war—and none of that scared him.

I can't let some poster scare me.

I walk over to Meghan. "Nice poster," I say. I don't want her to think I'm the tiniest bit scared by the Hart-Simon campaign. *Even though I kinda am.*

Meghan gives me a small smile. "It's just a campaign," she says, like she almost feels bad because she knows her poster is *that* good.

I just stand there, looking at her, because I'm not sure what to say next. And neither does she. We're having a silent conversation. What I'm saying: *I still can't believe we're running against each other.* Part of me thinks that's what she's saying, too. Part of me isn't sure.

Then Ben elbows me in the ribs. "C'mon, Adams," he says. "We have posters to put up and stickers to hand out."

And just like that my silent conversation with Meghan is over.

Ben and I start putting up our posters. We hand out stickers to any seventh grader we pass. The more we hand out, the better I feel. Meghan and Bree might wanna be president and vice president of our class, but Ben and I are gonna be.

Wannabes and Gonnabes. Two distinctly different groups. Ben and I belong in the second group. I'm sure about it.

But by the time the end of the school day rolls around, I'm not so sure about it. Everywhere I looked, seventh graders were wearing hot pink, heart-shaped stickers that read VOTE HART AND SIMON. Ben is waiting on the bench outside the gym where we agreed to meet before soccer practice, and I rush over to him. "Today was a disaster," I say.

Ben passes me a bag of chips and I pop one into my mouth. He pulls a clipboard from his backpack and delivers the bad news.

"My unofficial polls show that the Hart-Simon ticket has the support of girls' basketball, boys' football and basketball, the whole cross country team, the drama club, choir, mean girls, cool girls, cheerleaders, fashionistas, and social media influencers."

I rub the space between my brows. "I didn't know influencers were actually a group."

"They are. Six strong." Ben chugs from a bottle of blue Gatorade before continuing. "Chang-Robey have the honor society, band, orchestra, robotics team, math league, and an assortment of geeks, gamers, intellects, and book nerds on lockdown."

I frown. "So who does that leave for us? The foreign exchange students?"

Ben looks down at his clipboard. "Yep, both of them promised to vote for us. As did my fellow comedians. Don't laugh," he says.

I smirk. Nothing about this feels funny to me.

"Lighten up, Adams," chuckles Ben. "There are more kids than you'd think who believe that the school day goes more quickly when you find humor in it." I don't ask Ben how many kids that is exactly. Or if they're voting for us.

He keeps talking. "I hope we'll get the support of the boys' soccer team, which hasn't said which candidate they're backing. And we'll get votes from the guys in my band."

My brows shoot up. "You're in a band?"

"Was." Ben shrugs. "I got kicked out at our first practice. Something about not being good on vocals or any instruments. Anyway, the guys owe me one."

I shake my head. This race is turning into a who-likes-whom campaign, not who would do the best job. Though no one will have any way of knowing who that person might be until next week when all of the candidates are interviewed and make their speeches.

"Ben," I groan. "We need more supporters."

"Yep," says Ben. "And I have a plan to get some. We're going to target two groups. The first are what I call the *unaffiliateds,* Liberty Middle School seventh graders who don't play a sport or an instrument, aren't in any clubs, and can't be categorized."

I shake my head at Ben. Just about everyone I know does some kind of activity besides just going to class. "How many unaffiliateds are there?" I ask.

"Lots," says Ben. He jabs a finger at a list of names on his clipboard. "I'm going to call every name on this list personally and ask for their support." Ben takes out his phone and laptop from his backpack. "While I'm doing that, you need to get our second group on board."

I raise a brow at Ben.

"Every member of the girls' soccer team is still uncommitted," he says.

Just hearing that makes my heart race. Even though my teammates said they didn't want me to run, at least they haven't pledged their support for anyone else. That counts for something.

"I'm on it," I say, grabbing my backpack and heading to the field. I have a lot more to do at practice today than just making sure practice balls don't go flying into the net.

Chapter Twelve

ASK NOT WHAT YOUR TEAM CAN DO FOR YOU; ASK WHAT YOU CAN DO FOR YOUR TEAM

C oach Newton blows her whistle and everyone on my team sprints to huddle around her.

It's time for our post-practice, pregame pep talk. Coach Newton spends a few minutes doing a final review of some of our key plays, then says, "Girls, I know I don't have to tell you how important the game is tomorrow. This year we're going to beat Brookside!"

When Coach Newton says the name of Liberty's archrival, twenty-three fists are raised high into the air, and there's a long, loud chorus of boos and hisses.

"Brookside is the enemy," grunts Julie Jacobs, left midfielder and eighth-grade captain of our team. "They might have beaten us for the past three years, but we're not letting it happen again. Not us. Not this team. Let's send 'em back on their team bus crying like the whiny little babies that they are. GO LIBERTY!" she shouts, and the rest of the team starts chanting.

"GO LIBERTY! GO LIBERTY! GO LIBERTY!" Our words rise up like a battle cry.

Coach Newton motions for everyone to settle down. It takes a few minutes for the boos and hisses to stop, but when they finally do, she gives us all a serious look. "Girls, I want to share something I think is important and fitting for where we are as a team."

I zone out and think about the last talk I had with my teammates. When I brought up my campaign, none of them wanted to be my running mate.

Even worse, they didn't even want me to run. But if I'm going to win this election, I need their support. My soccer girls might not think I can block goals and run a campaign, but the time has come to convince them that that is **NOT** true. I refocus my attention on Coach Newton.

"Girls, President John F. Kennedy once said, 'Ask not what your country can do for you; ask what you can do for your country.'" She gives us a hard look. "Tomorrow at the game, I want you to ask yourselves not what your team can do for you, but what you can do for your team."

Funny how presidential wisdom is showing up in places other than my notebook.

Coach Newton lets her words sink in before continuing. "All I ask is that each one of you gives it your all in the game against Brookside tomorrow. Help each other. Work together. Can you do that?"

Our loud clapping and cheering is all the answer Coach needs. As my team starts to disperse, I fall into place beside Callie, Emily, Blake, and Zoey. The time has come for my talk.

"What's up?" Blake asks, like she can tell there's something on my mind.

Best to get straight to the point. "So, the last time I brought up the whole election thing, none of you were really that into it." All four of my teammates stop walking and look at me, so I continue. "I really need your support. This election is super important to me. And I promise you it won't get in the way of me playing good soccer."

Zoey shoots a look at the other girls. When they nod, she begins talking like she's the designated spokesperson. "Amanda, we get it. The election is important to you. But tomorrow's game is important to all of us."

I put my hands on my hips. It's so not fair to think the game isn't important to me just because the election is important, too.

I take a deep breath. I don't want to sound mad when I respond. "The game is important to me, too," I say slowly. "Brookside is our biggest rival."

Callie and Emily exchange a look.

"Sorry if we're being kind of tough," says Emily. "Of course you want to win, too."

"Yeah," I say. "I do. A lot."

Other seventh graders on the team are now clustered around us, and Callie picks up where Emily left off. "You know how much we all want to win tomorrow. And you play the most important position of anyone on our team. Brookside has a super strong offense, and it's up to you to stop them from making goals." She gives me a long, hard look. "We just want to be sure you'll be focused on the game tomorrow and not all of this election stuff."

"I will be."

But Emily shakes her head like she isn't convinced. "Look, Amanda, it's no secret that things have gotten pretty nasty between you and Meghan."

I blow out a breath. Ever since Meghan told me she was running against me, I've felt a mix of emotions. But what I'm feeling now is anger. Meghan keeps trying to one-up me. And now I'm the one who's paying the price. My own team doesn't even want to support me. I think about what Mom would do in this situation and straighten my shoulders.

"I've done my best to run a clean campaign. I can't control what other candidates do, and tomorrow I'll do my very best at the game. But I need your support, too," I say in the I-hope-I-can-count-on-you voice I've heard Mom use over and over again. "I can be a great goalie *AND* president of our class." My eyes lock with my teammates. "Can I count on you? All of you?"

There are murmurs. Then head nods.

Finally, an answer. "Fair is fair," says Callie. "Just block anything and everything that comes your way, and if you do, you have our support."

The word *if* is a scary one. Not quite what I wanted, but something is better than nothing. And blocking goals is my *thing*. I'm good at it. That's why Coach Newton made me goalie even though I'm only in seventh grade. And tomorrow, I'm going to be great at it.

"I got it!" I say confidently, then jog off. Tomorrow, it's all about what I can do for my team. And come voting day, it's going to be about what my team can do for me.

Chapter Thirteen
GOOD NEWS . . . OR NOT?

I close the door to my bedroom and open my laptop. I type in the words *John F. Kennedy*. Coach Newton got me thinking about our nation's thirty-fifth president. I want to look up his famous line, *"Ask not what your country can do for you; ask what you can do for your country."* But before I can read the results of my internet search, my phone rings.

It's Ben. "I have good news," he says, then tells me about the twenty-four unaffiliated kids in our class that he got to promise to vote for Adams and Ball as their class leaders.

"Are you kidding?" I squeal into the phone, then get up from my chair and happy dance around my room. "Seriously, Ben, great job! Great, great, great, great, great job!!!"

"Thanks," he says when I'm done with my *greats*. "But that's not all. I got the seventh-grade guys on the football team to promise to change their votes. And the seventh graders on the boys' soccer team agreed to support us, too."

I sink back into my chair. My fingers tighten around my phone. Something feels off here. "Ben, you're telling me that every seventh-grade boy on both the football and soccer teams promised they'd vote for us?"

"Bingo," says Ben.

Why would the football players, who were walking around campus today with pink, heart-shaped VOTE HART AND SIMON stickers stuck all over them, suddenly change their allegiance?

"Are you sure?" I ask, pretty certain Ben got this wrong.

He laughs into the phone. "Of course I'm sure."

My brain spins. None of this makes sense. "How'd you do it?"

"Ahh," says Ben, like finally I'm asking the right question. "The promise of my uncle's signature papaya smoothie is stronger than you can imagine. And don't worry," he adds before I have a chance to remind him of Mr. Ferguson's no-food rule. "Everything was done as a gentleman's agreement. No paper trail can be traced back to us. All people have to do is stop by the food truck and mention the secret code phrase: *I'm voting Adams and Ball.*"

I can practically feel Ben grinning into the phone. And I have to admit, I'm smiling, too.

"Wow!" I say. "That was easy. All you had to do was promise

free food to get the votes." I snap my laptop shut and prop my feet on my desk. "But it worked. So great!"

"Um, yeah, Adams, so there's one small detail I haven't shared with you yet."

My stomach rumbles, and I'm overcome by an ominous (a vocab word that means something bad or unpleasant is about to happen) feeling that whatever Ben is about to tell me isn't going to be something I want to hear.

"Ben . . ."

He clears his throat into the phone. "As you know, the game against Brookside tomorrow is a big one."

Of course, I know that. "Why are you reminding me?" I ask.

"Everyone will be at the game tomorrow," says Ben. "The boys' soccer team. The football team. They'll all be there cheering on Liberty against our archrival." He pauses, then adds, "All you have to do is make sure Brookside doesn't score, and their votes are yours."

I gulp. That was Ben's good news? To tell me that the outcome of tomorrow's game rests on my goalie shoulders? The only thing scarier than facing Brookside on the field is knowing that everyone in the stands will be counting on me to make sure they don't win the game. And that stopping them from scoring is the only way I can win the votes!

"Adams, you there?" Ben asks.

"Yeah," I say. "But stopping Brookside is a pretty tall order."

"Do you want the votes?"

Of course I do. "I'll do my best, but . . ." My voice trails off. I don't like thinking about what comes after the *but*. It goes something like this . . . *but if I fail, we're sunk. Toast. Doomed. Washed up before we even got started.*

"Just get out on that field tomorrow and don't let those nasty heathens score and we're golden. You can do it!" Ben sounds more like a cheerleader than a vice presidential hopeful.

"Sure," I say. Then I hang up.

I sure hope I can do it.

✳ ✳ ✳

MY CAMPAIGN INSPIRATION NOTEBOOK

✳ John F. Kennedy ✳

BORN: May 29, 1917, Brookline, Massachusetts

ASSASSINATED: November 22, 1963, in Dallas, Texas, by Lee Harvey Oswald

SIGN: Gemini. Traits: Thoughtful, articulate, entertaining, likeable.

PARTY: Democrat

STATUS: Married to Jackie Kennedy

KIDS: Two of them

PRESIDENCY: He became the 35th president of our nation in 1961

NICKNAME: JFK (Short and sweet!)

PETS: When JFK was president, the White House was like a zoo. During his administration, there were five horses, two parakeets, two hamsters, a cat, a rabbit, and five dogs at 1600 Pennsylvania Avenue.

COOL SKILL: He was a speed reader. He could read 1,200 words a minute, which is about 900 words a minute faster than most people read.

PLACES YOU CAN STILL FIND HIM: On the half-dollar

BIGGEST PRESIDENTIAL CHALLENGES: World peace and equal rights for all Americans.

KNOWN FOR: Being the youngest man elected president

ALSO KNOWN FOR: Being an inspiration to the nation

* * *

JFK wasn't president for long. Sadly, he was assassinated just three years into the job.

But while he was president, the world was a pretty crazy place. And he did lots of things to make it better. Cool things. If I had the time, I'd write about them here. Especially what he did in Cuba and to promote civil rights. But I don't have time. I have a lot of homework. *AND* a game tomorrow. So, if you want to look up JFK (You should!), you'll be amazed by what you read. The one thing I will say about him is that he said a lot of inspiring things, and right now I could use some serious inspiration (not only to win an election, but also a soccer game!).

So here goes.

Inspiring quote #1: "Ask not what your country can do for you; ask what you can do for your country."

Sound familiar? Yeah. I know. JFK said this in his inaugural address.

He challenged all Americans to contribute to the greater public good. Which I guess is no different than all players on a team working together for the win.

> *Inspiring quote #2: "Every decision starts with the decision to try."*

JFK faced lots of challenges during his presidency. He called his domestic program the New Frontier, and he made lots of promises to try to do things that had never been done. Like getting the first human on the moon. And getting important civil rights legislation passed.

I think JFK knew it wasn't going to be easy, but he wasn't afraid to try. I also think he knew he might fail, but that all he could do was his best.

> *Inspiring quote #3: "Only those who dare to fail miserably can achieve greatly."*

I'm pretty sure JFK wasn't the only one who said this. I think his brother, who was a senator, did too. And maybe some other presidents as well. Honestly, it sounds like something Dad would say. Or Mom. (Because Dad would have told her to say it.)

I get what it means: with big risk comes big reward. Running for president of my class against my best friend who has a very popular running mate is risky. So is being the starting goalie in seventh grade when lots of the girls I'm playing against are a year older and much bigger. But Coach Newton put me there for a reason.

What I need to remember is this: *If you don't take a big chance, you won't win.*

That's what I'm going to do tomorrow. When that final bell rings, I'm marching onto the soccer field and doing my best to make sure my team wins. I look in the mirror and give myself a pep talk. One I think JFK would have approved of.

I'm going to take a chance. I'm going to win. Go, Amanda! Go!

Chapter Fourteen

"AH LA VACHE!"
(IN ENGLISH: "OH MY COW!")

I stare at the back of Madame Moreau's head as she writes French expressions and the English translations on the board. Most of the expressions seem pretty useless. For example, *"Ah la vache."* Translated, it means "Oh my cow." Seriously?! Is there really a time when someone in France would have the need to say that?

Not that it matters. Right now, I have other, more important things on my mind.

Like the game against Brookside. I glance up at the clock in the front of the classroom. Only twelve minutes left of seventh period, then the school day ends and the game starts. I can honestly say that on the nerves scale, I'm way past ten. It's because this game against Brookside is the only thing everyone has been talking about.

ALL. DAY. LONG!

It started at breakfast, which actually took place in our kitchen as opposed to in our car. Dad scrambled eggs and Mom made a special protein smoothie for me. I didn't even know Mom knew how to make protein smoothies. "Amanda, I'll be at your game today," she said.

I gave her my best fake smile, like I was glad she'd be there. Which, to be honest, I'm not. The last time she came to one of my soccer games was last year when we played Brookside. And we lost. Call me superstitious, but she's not exactly our good luck charm.

Plus, having her there is a distraction. At least for me. That's because everyone in the stands will be looking at her and asking if they can take a selfie with the congresswoman from Virginia, then pointing to me because I'm the daughter of the congress-woman from Virginia. I get why people think taking a selfie with a congresswoman is cool, but Mom isn't Kim or Kanye.

"I'll be there too," Dad added, putting more scrambled eggs and a piece of toast on my plate. "And I can't wait to see our goalie in action."

"Thanks," I said, unsure what else to say.

Then, in homeroom, Mrs. Lee read an announcement about the soccer game after school and reminded everyone to come out and support the team against Brookside.

When she said the name of our archrival, the classroom

filled with boos, and Mrs. Lee whipped out a little blue-and-white pom-pom (I didn't even know she had one). "Go Liberty Girls' Soccer Team!" she said and pointed her cheering apparatus straight at me. "We're lucky to have our starting goalie in our midst. Amanda, anything you'd like to say?"

All eyes in the classroom settled on me, and I gulped. NO pressure there.

"We're going to kick some Brookside—"

Mrs. Lee cut me off before I could say what it was that we were going to kick. But she didn't look mad, and everyone was giving me fist bumps, so I flashed a smile.

"Go Liberty!" I said, hopeful I sounded confident.

The game against Brookside was the topic *du jour*. That's French for the only thing anyone was talking about all day.

At lunch, the J's were like . . . *we'll see you at the game today.*

And on my way to seventh period, I passed a group of seventh-grade football players who actually stopped me and said they were counting on me to stop Brookside.

"Got it," I said as I headed into French class.

Everyone knows it takes a team to win or lose a game, but I feel like this game is all on me. The thought makes my stomach knot up like a pretzel. I wonder if there's a French expression for that. Madame Moreau keeps writing, and my eyes wander.

Two rows up and one desk over is Meghan. In the desk next to her is Caleb Johannsen. Meghan is doing what she pretty much does every day in French class—crossing her right leg over her left. Then switching to left over right. Tucking her hair behind her ears. Straightening her mechanical pencils on her desk—anything to make it seem like she's not doing what she's really doing, which is looking at Caleb to see if he's looking at her.

No one else in the class would know what she's doing. Especially not Caleb.

But I know. Because there was a time when Meghan was my best friend and we knew EVERYTHING about each other. Now it's like we're practically strangers who barely even speak to each other. And today, I have the most important soccer game of my life.

Meghan knows how important it is that we beat Brookside.

Before this campaign started, she would have called me before school to be sure I was wearing my lucky socks. But today, the only thing she said to me about the game was *"Good luck."* And that was in homeroom after Mrs. Lee made her announcement and everyone was wishing me good luck.

Now, all she's doing is sitting there pretending she's not looking at the boy she has a crush on while I'm sitting here FREAKING OUT about the game. My armpits are sweaty, and I haven't even started warm-ups. I exhale, maybe too loudly, and Madame Moreau turns around. So does Meghan. Our eyes meet, and she flashes me a small smile, then twists back around in her seat.

Madame Moreau points to the first expression written on the board. "Translated, *Ah la vache* means 'Oh my cow.' But really it is the French way of expressing surprise or excitement."

I raise my hand and Madame Moreau calls on me. "What's the opposite of *Ah la vache*?" I ask. There must be an expression for expressing dread. As in, *I'm officially dreading this game.*

"That's a good question, Amanda." Madame Moreau purses her lips, which are painted an unflattering shade of fake fruit orange. It takes a while, but finally she answers.

"You could say *Zut alors*. Translated, it means *darn it.*"

The bell rings. *Darn it.* It's GAME TIME! In my entire thirteen-year life, I've never been more nervous. I take my time gathering my books, wishing I could turn back the clock and still be sitting at the breakfast table with Mom and Dad, eating eggs and toast. When a shadow covers my desk, I look up.

It's Meghan who flashes me a smile. "Good luck at the game. I'm sure you'll do great," she says sweetly. Then she adds, "I know you're probably nervous. But your nerves always disappear as soon as the game starts."

I exhale, feeling more confident than I have all day. Meghan is right. That's exactly what happens. "Are you going to be there?" I ask, suddenly realizing how much I want her to be.

"Sure," Meghan says. "Everyone will be there."

I gulp. *Zut alors.* And my game-day nerves shoot up to an all-time high.

Chapter Fifteen

THE TIME HAS COME TO KICK SOME BROOKSIDE YOU- KNOW-WHAT!

Let's go Liberty!"

Our team cheer echoes out from our pregame huddle and everyone who came to watch us play our nemesis shouts it right back.

I glance over the top of Callie Weaver's head and into the stands. I didn't think it was possible to cram so many people into the old metal risers that surround the Liberty Middle School field. The crowd on Liberty's side is overflowing. But there are just as many people on the opposite side of the field who came to cheer on Brookside. If this is what middle school soccer in Virginia is like, I can only imagine how it must feel to play in the World Cup.

I bend down to do a final check of the laces on my cleats. It's nice to think people care about our soccer team. But right now, I can't help but wish fewer did—especially people who are depending on me to shut down Brookside.

"Girls, we can do this," says Coach Newton. "Give it everything you got."

When I finish with my cleats, I look up and see that every eyeball of every member of the team is on me.

"Amanda, you ready?" asks Julie Jacobs, our team captain.

"I got it," I say (for what feels like the hundredth time today). The Brookside team is big and strong. I get that it's up to me to prevent them from scoring. But for me, beating Brookside is about more than just winning this game. It's about winning the election, too. Which is what's making me SOOOOO nervous. Except now isn't the time for nerves or to think about the election. I just have to stay focused on the game.

"Let's do this!" I shout; then all eleven of us—the starting players on our team—sprint out to take our positions on the field.

I take mine in front of the goal, and before the game starts, my eyes scan the crowd.

I locate Mom and Dad. Ben too. We make eye contact and he raises a militant fist in my direction. I know what it means. Win the game. Win the election.

My eyes keep moving over the crowd. I see Mrs. Lee. I'm not sure if my favorite teacher is here because she (a) is a big soccer fan, (b) wants to use her Liberty Middle School pom-pom, (c) is here to cheer me on, or (d) all of the above. Whatever. It's kind of comforting to see her face in the crowd.

I search for Meghan but don't see her anywhere. And don't have the time to keep looking. The Brookside girls are on the field, and the referee signals the start of the first half.

The ball is kicked from center circle and my stomach does an Olympic-style double backflip with a half twist.

Focus, I tell myself. What happens for the next thirty minutes is a blur. Players clad in blue jerseys (ours) and red jerseys (theirs) kick the ball up and down the field in front of supporters screaming at the top of their lungs for their respective teams.

I try to block out the noise and focus on one thing. The ball. More than a few times it hurtles toward me, and each time, I lunge, jump, or dive, doing my best to catch or block the ball and prevent Brookside from scoring. Then I pass it back to my teammates.

Each time I hear the roar of approval from the crowd. But I don't let it distract me. Surprisingly, my mind stays on one thing: doing my job.

But Brookside's goalie does her job, too. It's a hard-fought first half, and neither team scores. When the buzzer signals that it's time for the break before the second half, all of the players on both teams jog back to their benches.

I plop down on mine and wait for my breathing to steady.

"Great job, ladies," says Coach Newton.

Emily Peters slides onto the bench next to me. "Good work," she says.

"Yeah, awesome defense," adds Callie.

Other girls on the team voice their approval, too.

"Thanks," I breathe out, pleased by their compliments, but too winded to say much more.

I dig a bottle of Gatorade out of my gym bag, screw off the cap, and chug it down. As I drink, I see Ben in the stands waving and giving me a thumbs-up like I did a good job. Preventing Brookside from scoring was a lot of work. Now all I have to do is keep it up for another thirty minutes. I try not to think about what happens if I don't.

I wipe the sweat from my forehead with a towel while Coach Newton goes over our second-half plays and what she expects from both our offense and our defense.

"Stay focused," she warns when the buzzer sounds that ends the break. "And Amanda," she says, looking straight at me. "Watch out for air balls. It's what Brookside is known for."

"Will do," I say as I sprint back to my position.

The second half gets under way, and it's not any different from the first. Players move the ball up and down the field, with the support of the cheering crowd, but neither team scores. With just ten minutes remaining, the energy on the field and in the stands is supercharged.

So am I.

My arms and legs ache. Sweat drips down my forehead and back as I block and catch balls. But I don't care. When one of the biggest players on the Brookside team kicks the ball straight at our goal, I dive across the ground and use my entire body to deflect the shot.

The roar of the Liberty crowd fills my ears.

I look up at the clock. Less than two minutes to go, and so far I've done what I'm supposed to do: prevent Brookside from scoring.

My teammates pass the ball back down the field. It goes from Julie to Emily, who is dribbling it toward the Brookside goal. I will my team to score. If we do, I'll have the game and a whole lot of votes in the bag. I can practically taste the victory.

I relax, just for a second, and glance up into the stands.

That's when I see it: Meghan and the J's. They're all sitting there, looking at something on their phones and laughing. Not one of them is watching the game, and I feel a flash of anger.

How can Meghan sit there looking at Instagram while I'm down here trying to help my team win the most important game of the season? And what kind of a friend does that make her that she doesn't even care enough to watch and cheer me on? On the mad scale, I'm a ten!

Then I hear my name being shouted. "AMANDA!"

And faster than I can react to what's happening on the field, an air ball goes sailing right over my head and into the goal. The roar of the crowd fills my ears.

But it isn't coming from the Liberty side of the field. The fans in the Brookside bleachers are going CRAZY, and my stomach goes into free fall.

There's only a minute and a half left to play. I say a silent prayer that somehow my team will score, but when the buzzer sounds, it's a prayer that has fallen into the unanswered category.

I look down at my cleats, too afraid to look at the disappointed faces of my teammates. Or Coach. Or the fans in the stands. And unable to watch the Brookside players doing their victory dance. One second, maybe two or three, was the amount of time that I lost my focus. Three teensy, tiny little seconds. *One one-thousand. Two one-thousand. Three one-thousand.*

In that short little window of time, my team lost the game.

And quite possibly, I lost an election.

Chapter Sixteen
I'M FINE . . . FINE. FINE. FINE. FINE. FINE.

I 'm fine," I tell my parents. *Fine. Fine. Fine. Fine. Fine.*

They exchange a worried look, then Dad sips from his soda and puts his glass down on the table. It makes a loud *thunk* sound.

"Amanda, that's eight *fines* since we sat down. What's going on?"

I stuff my mouth with pizza. Papa Rocco's mushroom and pepperoni pizza. My favorite pizza in Arlington. If I were stranded on a deserted island and could only take one food, it would definitely be Papa Rocco's mushroom and pepperoni pizza. But now I'm eating it not because it tastes good. It's a stall tactic. With my mouth full, there's no way I can answer Dad's question.

The one about what's going on with me.

There are some things a seventh-grade girl just doesn't want to discuss with her parents. Like that she just lost the biggest soccer game of the season, has a whole team of girls mad at her, and got a long lecture from her coach about staying focused during the WHOLE game, and that if she doesn't at the next game, she's out as starting goalie. Not to mention she's about to lose an election to her ex–best friend. Which Meghan so is. Especially after today's game. I just don't get how she could sit there looking at her phone while I was trying to win a game.

Mom nibbles the crust from her slice of pizza and studies me.

"Amanda, I know my daughter," she finally says. "And I know something is bothering you. You can tell me right now or . . ."

I clamp my lips shut and wait for option B.

"Or I can guess," Mom adds. "Is this about the game? The election?" She glances at Dad like she's looking for his approval before saying what comes next. He gives a small nod, and she adds, "Or what's happening with Meghan? Honey, she's your best friend and I know that having her as an opponent doesn't feel good."

I sigh. "Fine," I say.

"No more *fines*!" Mom and Dad grunt at the same time.

I push away my plate. I didn't mean *fine* as in *I'm fine*. More like, *Fine, I'll start talking.* Telling my parents everything that's wrong can't make me feel any worse than I already do.

"It's all of the above," I say. Then I start by telling my parents about everything that has happened with Meghan. And how she came to the game today but wasn't even watching.

I sigh. "Ever since the campaign started, all of our friends are now *her* friends. She's always with them and her running mate, Bree. Seriously, it's like they're glued to her side." I shoot Dad a helpless look. "Remember the talk you wanted me to have with her?"

Dad nods.

"Well, there was no way I could have it, because she's never alone!"

Mom shakes her head. "I know how hard it can be when things with your best friend aren't right. But I have a feeling you girls will work through your differences."

"Um, Mom, I'm not so sure about that." A best friend gone AWOL (a military term I learned in Social Studies that means "absent without official leave," or away from one's post) makes me wish more than ever I had a dog that could curl up on my lap and look at me with eyes that say *Don't worry, you'll always have me.* Now seems as good a time as any to remind my parents how much I want one. "I'd probably feel a whole lot less bad about what's happening with Meghan if I had a dog," I say.

My parents exchange a look I can't quite read. "Amanda, let's stick to the election conversation. How is your campaign going?" Dad asks.

I frown. "Awful! Meghan's campaign posters and stickers were soooooo much better than mine. And there's the issue of who is voting for whom."

I tell Mom and Dad about the groups in my grade promising to vote for Frankie, the ones supporting Meghan, and how Ben got people to promise to vote for me if I stopped Brookside from beating Liberty.

"I didn't do it. And now there's no way I'm going to win this election." I stare down at my plate. "Even the girls on my team aren't going to vote for me." I think about the "we told you so" conversation they had with me after the game. Not my idea of fun.

"Yes, they will," says Mom.

"No," I look up to correct her. "They won't. They didn't want me to run in the first place because they didn't think I could play good soccer AND run for office." I blow out a breath. "And they were right. It's my fault we lost the game."

The server returns to our table to refill our water glasses. When she's done, Dad gives me a *father-knows-best* look. "Kids will still vote for you even though Liberty lost the game. And I know you'll find a way to get the support of your teammates."

"No," I say to Dad. "I won't. I'm the reason my team lost,

and everyone knows it. I'm not just talking about the girls on my team. I'm talking about EVERYONE in my grade!"

"Have you heard the term *yesterday's news*?" asks Dad. "People have short memories. By next week, they won't even remember the soccer game."

I shake my head. *They'll definitely remember.*

"Amanda . . ." Mom says my name in her *I'm-about-to-make-an-important-statement* voice, but I interrupt before she can say more.

"Mom, no one is going to forget about the most important game of the season. I don't think you understand: NO ONE wants me to be president of the seventh grade."

I prop my elbows on the table and let my chin fall into my hands. "I'm toast."

I see Dad biting back a smile as he motions for the check. "Amanda, I'm about to teach you an important rule of all campaigns: it's not over until it's over."

"Your father is right," adds Mom. "Do you have any idea how many campaigns I was certain I was going to lose up until the very last vote was counted?"

"None?" I guess. Mom never loses. She never even comes close to losing.

My answer makes both of my parents laugh out loud and the people in the next booth look at us like they want to know what's so funny.

"Amanda, your mother has been in more close elections than I can count," says Dad. "Even people who promise to vote for a candidate often don't. But as campaigns come to a close, things have a funny way of happening that persuade voters to change their minds."

I scratch at a mosquito bite on my wrist. "What kinds of things are you talking about?"

Dad leans forward as he speaks. "All you've done so far is hang posters and pass out stickers. Those things set the tone of your campaign. But they're not nearly as important as what your campaign is really about. What will you do as class president?"

I get what Dad is saying. "Interviews with the candidates are on Tuesday," I say. "And speeches are Thursday morning before the voting."

"Great!" says Dad. "That gives you two opportunities to share your platform with your classmates." He picks up a spoon from the table and sticks it in front of me like it's a microphone. "Amanda Adams, what would you do as president of the seventh grade?"

Ben and I have talked a lot about this, which means it's a question I can answer. I sit up straighter in my chair and lean over Dad's mock microphone.

"I'll start a petition for longer lunches." I lay out my plan for Mom and Dad about how I plan to lobby Principal Ferguson to add five more minutes to lunch. It sounds like a small thing, but anyone (and that would be every single student at my school) who has had to throw down their lunch to get to their next class on time knows what a difference five minutes would make.

"I like that idea," says Dad.

Mom smiles. "Me too."

"Yeah," I say. "A lot of kids will. Ben and I talked to almost everyone in our grade to see what issues are important to them. The jocks want the track resurfaced. The brass section of the band wants new instruments. The photo club thinks they need a new darkroom. And the vegan club wants a ban on junk food in the vending machines. The two things *everyone* we talked to wanted were a Starbucks on campus and longer lunches."

Dad smiles. "Sounds to me like you're backing the right issue."

"I think so," I say. "Hopefully Principal Ferguson will agree to longer lunches. I'd feel bad promising something and then not delivering it."

"Amanda, another cardinal rule of campaigns is to never EVER promise something that you're not sure you can deliver," says Dad. "You can promise to try."

"Got it," I say. I understand the difference.

Our server returns to our table with the check and three peppermints. I pop one into my mouth and give my parents a grateful smile. "Thanks for your help," I tell them.

"Glad we could be of assistance," says Mom. "Just remember . . . the days leading up to voting day can be the most stressful."

"She's right," says Dad. "Be prepared for whatever might come your way."

I roll my eyes. I'll admit that something could go wrong when you get interviewed on school TV and have to make a speech in front of your whole grade.

But nothing can be worse than losing the soccer game and knowing you let down your entire team AND school. Or enduring the stares and mumbles that came my way after I did. Most of them were behind my back, but it made me feel like I had a giant "L," for loser, posted on my chest. Even worse was my talk with Coach Newton after the game. She was crystal clear when she warned me that I have one shot at redemption or I'm O-U-T as starting goalie.

I shudder just thinking about it.

I can't rewrite history. But what I can do is focus on the future.

Ben and I spent a lot of time finding the most important issue to campaign on. Tomorrow, he's coming over and we're working on what I'm going to say at the interview and in my speech.

Bottom line: Nothing that happens next week can be as bad as what happened this week.

Right? *Right!*

Chapter Seventeen

IF IT LOOKS LIKE A DOG AND BARKS LIKE A DOG, IT STILL MIGHT NOT BE A DOG

It's Monday afternoon. Fifth-period science class. I try to focus on what Mrs. Lee is saying about the supplies for our charcoal water purifying experiment, but that's not so easy to do. Not when my lab partner keeps talking about what happened at last week's soccer game. So much for Dad's *yesterday's news* theory.

"You must have been pretty upset," Meghan says.

"Um, yeah," I say, stating the obvious. I'm not sure if she's trying to make me feel better or worse. I glance over at her for a clue.

Meghan's wearing the jean jacket I persuaded her to buy. The one with little silver studs all over it. I remember the day she found it at the mall and I told her it was *soooo* her and she had to get it. I also remember the day we talked Mrs. Lee into making us lab partners and gave her our solemn promise we would spend our time in the lab experimenting, not talking. Then I couldn't keep my mouth shut. Now I don't feel like opening it.

"Amanda." Her mouth starts to move like she has something more to say, but before she has the chance, Mrs. Lee calls on me.

"Amanda, do you and Meghan have a pre-experiment hypothesis?" she asks.

"We do," I say. Meghan and I might not be best friends, but we're still A+ lab partners. We both love science, and even before we both wanted to be president of our class, we wanted to be famous scientists. We even had ideas for things we wanted to invent—gummy bears that make you remember everything you learn so you're always prepared for pop quizzes, and an aerosol spray that prevents bad hair days and pimples.

Our love of science will never change. But other things have changed a whole, whole lot.

"Our pre-experiment hypothesis is that charcoal can remove molecules from water," I say. "This is based on our previous knowledge that charcoal filters are used to clean water."

"Good work," says Mrs. Lee.

Meghan gives me a thumbs-up, even though we both know the analysis was a simple one. We both have Brita pitchers in our refrigerators at home, which use carbon filters.

Mrs. Lee is talking, and I force myself to focus on her directions for our experiment.

Fill a measuring cup with ½ cup of water.

Add eight drops of red food coloring and stir until mixed.

Divide the colored water into two baby food jars.

In one jar, add two teaspoons of activated carbon.

Set the jars aside and check them each day for three days for color changes.

When Mrs. Lee is done talking, Meghan and I start prepping for our experiment. Usually when we prep, we talk. That's almost always when Mrs. Lee has to remind us that we're in class. But today, Meghan and I fill our baby food jars and neither of us says a word.

Whatever Meghan was going to say before Mrs. Lee called on me, she doesn't. And I don't say anything, either. It feels weird to be so quiet during lab. But it's like neither of us is sure what to say.

When we're done, we label our jars *A & M* and put them on the observation shelf.

Back at our lab station, Meghan clears her throat and instinctively I look up. "So, are you ready for the interview tomorrow?" she asks.

I think of Ben and the mock interview he did with me on Saturday so that I'll be ready for whatever our on-air class reporter, Stella O'Shea (aka Casey Lieberman), asks me on Tuesday morning.

"I'm ready," I tell her.

Meghan bites her lip. "Amanda, I don't want to say too much, but I wouldn't be a good friend if I didn't tell you that I have a surprise I'm going to announce tomorrow. It's **BIG**. And I'm pretty sure everyone's going to love it." She shrugs. "Just thought you should know."

A hot feeling of anger shoots along my spine. I don't see how Meghan telling me that she has a **BIG** surprise makes her a good friend.

She's being the opposite of a good friend. She's being a word that starts with *B* and rhymes with *witch*. I know Meghan, and I know exactly what she's trying to do. She's trying to get in my head. Scare me before the interview. She probably doesn't even have a surprise.

One of Dad's favorite expressions comes to me. Funny enough, it's about dogs. He likes to say: *If it looks like a dog and barks like a dog, it's a dog.* In my case, Meghan might look like my best friend and talk like my best friend, but she's definitely not my best friend.

Not anymore.

The bell rings and I grab my books and hurry off to my

next class, English. I spot Ben in the hallway and rush over to him. When I tell him what Meghan said, his ears perk up.

"What do you think the surprise is?" he asks.

I groan, frustrated. Ben doesn't know Meghan like I do. "Don't you get it?" I wave my hands dramatically through the air. "She's playing me. There's no **BIG** surprise."

Ben motions for me to calm down. "Adams, let's consider the possibility that she has something up her sleeve."

I raise a brow at Ben. "Like what? Besides her elbow. What's bigger than longer lunches?"

Ben shrugs. "Dunno. But what if she has something that is?"

"We've got something," I remind Ben. "Two somethings. An awesome idea for our class community service project. And a great theme for the dance."

Ben frowns. "But what if she drops a major bombshell?"

He doesn't wait for me to answer. Just claps his hands together and makes a loud *KABOOM* sound. A group of sixth-grade girls in front of us scatters like scared mice.

"Ben, there's nothing Meghan can say or do that will hurt us." Not in the way he's thinking. "Breathe," I say, imitating a yoga teacher I once saw on TV.

Ben snort-laughs. "Adams, I'm a comedian. Not a yogi. Hey, do you know how you make a tissue dance?"

"Huh?" I ask, surprised by the sudden turn in the conversation.

"Put a little boogie in it," Ben says.

"Ew! Ben, that's gross." Still, I give him a half smile, which turns to a smirk when I see Bree and Jayda at the end of the hallway, passing out more of Meghan's campaign hearts.

Who knows what Meghan has up her sleeve for this interview? But whatever it is, I'm going to be ready for her!

MY CAMPAIGN INSPIRATION NOTEBOOK

✳ Richard Nixon ✳

BORN: January 9, 1913, Yorba Linda, California

DIED: April 22, 1994, at a hospital in New York

SIGN: Capricorn. Traits: Adaptable, hardworking, determined.

PARTY: Republican

STATUS: Married to Patricia Nixon

KIDS: Two girls, Julie Nixon Eisenhower and Tricia Nixon Cox

PRESIDENCY: He became the 37th president of our nation in 1969

NICKNAME: Tricky Dick (Go ahead, laugh. I did!)

PETS: Three dogs. Vicky (poodle), Pasha (terrier), and King Timahoe (Irish setter)

IMPRESSIVE FACT: Nixon couldn't read music, but he could play five instruments: piano, sax, accordion, clarinet, and violin.

SAD FACT: He was the only president to ever resign from office.

At dinner tonight, Mom asked how the campaign was going. I told her what Meghan said about her **BIG** surprise announcement, and that even though most of me isn't worried about whatever it is she might say, part of me wants to be ready just in case. Mom made a *tssk* sound and said big didn't always equal good when it came to announcements. Then she said I should read about the one Richard Nixon made on August 9, 1974.

So here goes.

Richard Nixon was elected president in 1969 after serving as a U.S. Representative and a U.S. Senator from California. He did a lot of good things while he was president. Like ending American fighting in Vietnam. And improving relations with Russia and China. But then something bad happened: Watergate. To make a long story very short, it was a major political scandal that went all the way up to the President of the United States.

It started in 1972 when five men broke into the headquarters of the Democratic National Committee to steal information. When they were caught, the Nixon administration tried to cover up their involvement. But the thing about secrets is that they don't always stay secret, and in this case they didn't. Watergate was investigated by the FBI and Congress. A bunch of people were arrested. And finally, impeachment proceedings (that means the process to kick a president out of office) began. But before they got too far, Nixon announced that he was resigning the presidency. That was the **BIG** announcement Mom was talking about.

But honestly, I don't see how this relates to whatever it is that Meghan is going to announce. She can't get impeached. She hasn't even been elected.

I keep reading about Nixon to see if he did anything that might inspire me. Finally, I find one thing. But it didn't happen when Nixon was president. It happened in 1952 when he was running as the Republican vice presidential candidate. And the cool thing about this story is that it had to do with his puppy. A cocker spaniel named Checkers.

During the campaign, Nixon was accused of misusing some of his political expense fund. Dwight Eisenhower, his running mate, wanted to drop him from the ticket. But Nixon defended himself before a live TV and radio audience of sixty million people (that's a whole lot more than the 172 kids in my grade who will be listening to me tomorrow), saying he'd done nothing wrong with the money.

Then he brought up Checkers. The puppy was a gift from one of his campaign supporters, and Nixon's six-year-old daughter was in LOOOOVE! Nixon said they were keeping Checkers, and his speech became known as the "Checkers" speech.

It saved Nixon's career. He was betting on the fact that most people believed that any man who loved dogs couldn't be all bad. Eisenhower kept him on the ticket, and Nixon went on to be elected vice president, then president.

Nixon had a dark side. He did some bad things. Some good things too. He sure knew how to use the media to his advantage. And that was before Twitter and Instagram even existed!

I think the lesson here is that tomorrow, when I'm interviewed, I need to do what Nixon did: use the media to my advantage and say something people want to hear.

Who knows what the **BIG** thing is that Meghan might (or might not) announce.

But it doesn't matter. I know what I'm going to say. (Unfortunately, it's not that someone gave me a puppy and I'm keeping it.)

I'm going to say that I'll be fighting for longer lunches.

And that for our class community service project, we're going to have a book drive *and* build a kid-run library. Not from the ground up, with bricks, wood, and cement. But we're going to find a room somewhere and turn it into a place where kids from all over Arlington can come to check out cool books other kids have read. And kids can even take turns being librarians.

And for our class dance we're going to have a Vegas-themed party with casino tables and cool prizes.

Come tomorrow, when Stella O'Shea (aka Casey Lieberman) interviews me, I'm going to do what Nixon did and tell the people all of these things.

Things I know they'll want to hear.

Chapter Eighteen
LIGHTS. CAMERA. START TALKING.
(OR, SOME THINGS ARE BETTER LEFT UNSAID)
(OR: #BEACHBOUND)

INTERIOR SCENE: A nondescript room next to Principal Ferguson's office filled with A/V and lighting equipment. Sign on the wall reads: "Home of the Liberty Middle School TV station." In a chair sits seventh-grade reporter Casey Lieberman, also known by her on-air persona of Stella O'Shea. Despite the fancy name, Stella looks like your average middle schooler, with crooked bangs, braces, and beat-up sneaks. Across from her sit the three candidates who are running for class president: Meghan Hart, Frankie Chang, and Amanda Adams.

CAMERAMAN (to everyone in room)

We're rolling in five . . . four . . . three . . . two . . . one . . . and we're live!

Bright lights switch on. All three candidates blink, then focus on the microphone in Stella's hand.

STELLA (looking into camera)

Good morning, fellow seventh graders. I'm Stella O'Shea broadcasting live with our very own class presidential candidates. The big election is two days away, and this morning I'm bringing the candidates into your homerooms so we can all get a sneak peek into the issues that move them most. I'll start with Frankie Chang. Tell us, Frankie, if elected, what would you do to make a difference for your fellow classmates?

A small boy who looks like he belongs in the elementary school down the road pushes his glasses up on his nose. His shirt is buttoned to his neck. His facial expression is serious. He pulls a notecard from his shirt pocket and begins to read.

FRANKIE (from a notecard)

If elected, I will work to ensure that every student in our class is given an extra study hall during the school day. That way kids will have less work to do at home and more time at night for things they want to do. Like play video games. Or write code.

STELLA (nods, like she's impressed)

Interesting. I'm sure you'll get a lot of votes on the less-homework-at-night thing. And tell us, Frankie, do you have any ideas for the class community service project and a theme in mind for the dance?

FRANKIE (from another notecard)

For the community service project, my plan is to collect old eyeglasses and distribute them to people in need.

Frankie adjusts his own glasses, then continues without a notecard.

FRANKIE

To be honest, I'm only ten and I've never been to a dance. So I really don't have any ideas about it.

STELLA (fighting back a smile)

Totally understandable. Thank you for your honesty, Frankie, and good luck.

Stella O'Shea turns her attention to the remaining two candidates.

STELLA (to Meghan)

Now on to Meghan Hart. Meghan, you've waged an impressive campaign so far. It's no secret your contraband donuts were a hit. So was the big sign outside the cafeteria. And those cute little pink heart stickers. Nice touch! But what our fellow classmates want to know is how Meghan Hart will make a difference.

Meghan leans forward in her chair. She tucks a strand of blond hair behind her right ear, smiles into the camera, then begins to speak.

MEGHAN (sweetly)

Thanks for your question, Stella. I feel I'd make a huge difference. I'm all about what I call "The S's." That's short for snacks and spirit. As president, I'd make sure we have lots more of both.

STELLA

Sounds great. Everyone likes snacks and spirit. And tell us, do you have ideas in mind for the community service project and the dance?

Before speaking, Meghan glances at the remaining candidate, who experiences a sudden chill, even though the lights in the TV station make the room they're in very HOT.

MEGHAN

The community service project and the dance are both a HUGE deal, and this year what I want to do is combine them. My idea is that we go as a class to nearby Sandy Point State Park and clean up the beach. Once we're done, we can have our dance there. It would be really fun. Music. Swimming. Dancing. Roasting hot dogs and s'mores. I even have a name for it . . .

Meghan looks into the camera and her glossy pink painted lips form the words "#beachbound."

STELLA (smiling really big)

Wow! I love that! And I'm sure lots of our fellow classmates would agree that "#beachbound" sounds like a great way to combine community service and fun.

Stella turns her attention to the one remaining candidate, who has a sudden, AWFUL feeling, like she's been pushed out of an airplane with no parachute. All of the on-air tips her mother gave her last night, like sit up straight, don't fidget, and NEVER wear horizontal stripes, seem unhelpful when she knows that what she really needs is an idea that is MUCH better than a book drive or a kid-run library or a Vegas-themed party.

STELLA (to Amanda)

Amanda Adams, you're our final candidate. Tell us how you would make a difference.

Amanda sits up straight. She doesn't fidget. And she isn't wearing horizontal stripes. She has on the mint green sweater her mother chose for her. She smiles into the camera, hopeful that she appears calmer than she looks as she delivers her first answer.

AMANDA

Thanks for having us here today, Stella. I'm all about making a difference for our class. And the place I would start would be with longer lunches. Every student at Liberty Middle School knows that awful feeling of throwing down their lunch to get to their next class in time.

STELLA (laughing)

Safe to say we all know that feeling. Cheers to you if you can get Principal Ferguson to go along with your plan. Now tell us your plans for the community service project and the dance.

Amanda smiles into the camera even though she has nothing to smile about. She thinks about Nixon and how he got elected by telling the people what they wanted to hear. She tries to think of something she can say that the people want to hear. Something more exciting than a book drive or a student-run library. But she can't think of one single thing. Her only choice is to tell her classmates what she has planned.

AMANDA

For our community service project, I want to do a book drive of teen books, then start a teen-run library where kids from all over Arlington can come to check out books recommended by their peers. Kids could even take turns being the librarians. And my idea for the dance is to have a Vegas-themed party with casino tables and cool prizes.

STELLA (stifling a yawn)

That's nice. And that's a . . .

But before she can say "wrap" like she always says when she signs off, an idea pops into Amanda's head and she spits it out before she has time to think about the reasons why she shouldn't.

AMANDA

Stella, I'd like to add one more thing, if you don't mind.

Stella gives Amanda a look like she does mind, but Amanda keeps talking anyway.

AMANDA (looking directly into camera)

As many of you know, my mother is a congresswoman from the great state of Virginia. And if I'm elected president of our class, she has promised to take our whole grade on an insiders' tour of the Capitol.

STELLA (to Amanda)

WOW! I'm sure every seventh grader out there would agree that's super cool.

STELLA (continuing to talk directly into camera to audience)

Wow! An inside view of our nation's Capitol Building is on my bucket list, and I'm betting it's on yours, too. And with that awesome campaign promise, that's a wrap.

The lights dim and the cameraman turns off the camera equipment. All three candidates hurry off to their first-period classes, but one of them has a pit in her stomach the size of the state of Virginia (actually, it's the size of a much bigger state, like Texas). And that's because she's just made a campaign promise she's not sure she can keep.

Chapter Nineteen
FOR EVERY ACTION, THERE'S A REACTION
(AND IN THIS CASE, LOTS OF THEM!)

REACTION #1: BEN'S

Ben is waiting for me when I walk out of the TV station, and he's grinning like he just delivered a perfectly timed punch line.

"Adams, you killed it in there! It's so cool that the Honorable Congresswoman Adams agreed to take our class on a field trip. Like everyone in my homeroom can't wait to go. I mean, with that one sentence, you next-levelled things. Adams and Ball are going straight to the highest office in the class!" Ben gives me a hearty pat on the back. "Good job in there!" he says, and then his nose wrinkles up like a pug's. "But why didn't you tell me about it?"

That's a great question. But answering it honestly makes me hot and itchy inside my mint green sweater. "Um, yeah. About that . . ."

We pass one boy in my class who gives me a thumbs-up and another who says, "#capitolbound!" I give them friendly waves, then lean closer to Ben. No one but him needs to hear what I'm about to say next. "My mom didn't agree to it," I whisper. "I made it up."

"WHAAAAAT???"

Ben's question is an eight on the loudness scale, and I motion to him to keep it down.

"I didn't mean to make it up, but when Meghan brought up the whole beach thing, I knew I needed something really good. Like a *pièce de résistance*." Ben looks confused, so I explain. "That's French for something so good, everyone will vote for us."

"Got it," says Ben; then he frowns. "So you volunteered your mom for a Capitol tour to get votes. Brilliant. If it works. Think she'll do it?"

I sigh. "I think she's going to be upset I volunteered her for something like that without asking first. And that I made a campaign promise I might not be able to keep."

Two girls from my PE class high-five me as we pass in the hall.

"Great job on TV," says Kat Hale.

Autumn McKinley tells me she's always wanted to visit the Capitol.

I shake my head at Ben. "I made a promise I can't break. I'm going to have to figure out how to tell my mom what I did and get her on board."

The bell rings, signaling the start of first period, but Ben just stands outside his classroom chewing on his lip like he's thinking. I need to know what's on his mind before I walk into Mr. Corbett's class or there's no way I'll be able to spend the next forty-five minutes focused on algebraic equations. "What?" I ask.

"Adams, if your mom is going to be upset when she hears it from you, imagine how she'll feel if she hears if from someone else first. My advice: figure out how to tell her, and do it FAST!"

REACTIONS #2 AND #3: MOM'S AND DAD'S

As soon as Mom walks in the front door, I greet her with a cold glass of Diet Snapple Peach Tea (her favorite) and some good news. "Mom, I cleaned my room," I say.

Mom accepts the tea, then sinks into an armchair in our den and gives me a tired smile. "Happy to hear it."

"Did I hear something about a clean room?" Dad appears in the den without warning, then furrows his brows at me. "Amanda, you hate cleaning your room."

That's true. I do hate cleaning my room. Mom and Dad are now BOTH looking at me like they suspect I had a cleaning motive. Better just to get this over with. I cross my toes inside my sneakers and make a wish that this talk will go well.

Slowly I tell my parents what happened in the interview. When I get to the part about the tour, Mom shrieks my name.

"AMANDA! Nixon was meant to be a cautionary tale. Not an example." She shakes her head. "How could you promise something like that without asking me first?"

Dad doesn't give me a chance to answer. He immediately starts in on how it was wrong. How I put Mom in a difficult position. That she has a civic duty to represent all middle school classes in her district. Not just her daughter's. And that the logistics of this sort of thing are complicated.

"Your mother can't play the favorite middle school game," Dad says.

A lump forms in my throat. I hadn't thought about that.

"Mom, I'm sorry. Really sorry. But I need your help." My voice cracks as I talk. "I know what you and Dad told me about never making promises I can't keep. But I won't win this election if I don't have something better than a beach party."

Mom and Dad exchange a look.

"Amanda, Mom and I need to discuss this," says Dad in his *campaign-strategist-doing-damage-control* voice. His words are low and scary, especially to me.

I nod. That's my cue that Mom and Dad have said all they're going to say for now.

I get up and go to my (clean) room. A tear trickles down my cheek. Followed by another. And another. This whole campaign thing has gotten so out of hand. It seems like a very long time ago that I was excited to declare my candidacy. So many bad things have happened since then. My best friend decided to run against me. I lost the most important soccer game of the season and let down my teammates and my coach and my school. Now, my parents are mad at me, too.

Seriously . . . can it get any worse?

REACTION #4: MEGHAN'S

I stare at the screen of my laptop, trying to process Meghan's latest Instagram post.

It's a picture of me shaking hands with Stella after the interview and a caption that reads: "Don't believe everything you hear on TV. A Capitol tour? Hmmm. Really??? I would know. #nothappening #beachbound"

I slam my computer shut and grab my phone. "Did you see what she posted?" I ask as soon as Ben answers.

"Yep. And so did a lot of other people."

Comments on Meghan's post are appearing faster than I can down a Gatorade after practice on a hot day. I read some of them aloud to Ben.

How do you know?

Is she lying?

Can AA deliver on her promise???

I growl into the phone. "This is bad," I say to Ben. "My ex–best friend is basically calling me a liar!" As I watch the comments pile up, I realize lots of people believe her.

"No one wants a liar as their president," I fume. "And the worst part is that Meghan doesn't know if it's true or not."

"Exactly!" says Ben like I've made his point. "It might *not* be true."

"Yeah," I say. "If I can find a way to get Mom to agree to it."

"Adams, where there's a will there's a way. Stay focused and finish your speech. Then put your head into figuring out how to persuade your mom to go along with the plan."

"Will do," I say to Ben.

What I don't say: This is war. And Meghan started it.

REACTION #5: MINE!

I stay focused just long enough to finish my speech, which Mrs. Lee is expecting to see on her desk first thing tomorrow morning. I still don't have a solution to the biggest problem on my list: getting Mom to let me keep the promise I made that she'll take my class on a tour of the Capitol if I win the election.

But to be honest, right now I can't stop checking Instagram to see who else liked or commented on Meghan's post.

Every time I look, I just get madder. Not just about the post. But about everything that's happened since the campaign started.

It's almost like there are two Meghans. The one who's been my best friend since the first day of first grade and who likes to do fun things together, like go to the mall and conduct science experiments. The one who knows things about me that no one else does—like that I get nervous before a game, but that my nerves go away when the game starts.

Then there's the other Meghan. The one who decided to run against me for president of our class and planned it all behind my back. The one who picked Bree as a running mate, got the J's to work on her campaign, and ordered special T-shirts and donuts. The one who came to my game but didn't even watch, and now is calling me a liar!

One of dad's favorite expressions is *Every action has an equal but opposite reaction.* Come to think of it, I'm pretty sure Mrs. Lee said exactly the same thing when we were doing a science experiment in the lab. Sooooo if Meghan calls me a liar, don't I have the right to react?

The answer is simple. YES, I DO! Then a genius plan pops into my brain.

Meghan isn't the only one who can post on Instagram.

I scroll through Meghan's texts until I find the photo she sent me from the last football game. It's of Caleb J running off the field. I remember when she took it. We were sitting next to each other in the stands, cheering like crazy, and Meghan was trying not to look like she was taking a picture of Caleb. But she did.

I click on it.

I enlarge and edit the picture so it's mostly just a blurry jersey. But the number 23 is easy to see. I post the photo on Instagram with the caption: "A certain seventh-grade prez hopeful with blond highlights has a favorite number. #no lie"

As soon as I post it, I get this weird feeling in my stomach. Like maybe what I did wasn't such a good idea. I think about GW's *Rules of Civility* and what he would have had to say about revealing your ex-bestie's deepest, darkest secret on Instagram. Not to mention that she got highlights.

George would be like: *"Insta-what?"* Social media was way before his time, so his opinion really doesn't matter here.

What's done is done. I can't undo it. And another thing Dad always says is that first instincts are always right and to listen to them. Well, that's what I did.

I think about Nixon. He wasn't afraid to use the media. And I'm not either. I turn off my phone and my light.

Then I go to sleep.

Chapter Twenty

A WHOLE LOT OF WRONGS DON'T MAKE IT RIGHT

(OR, THE BATTLE OF THE EX-BESTIES)

My alarm sounds and I blink open my eyes. For two sleepy seconds, it's just like any other morning. But then I remember what I did last night, and I'm hit with a vision of Meghan's face reacting to my post, and it's not a pretty picture.

Who wouldn't be upset if an (ex) best friend spilled the beans on your secret crush. I can just see Meghan calling Bree and then the J's, and I'm sure they were all like, "OMG, I can't believe Amanda did that!! Bad Amanda. Bad. Bad. Bad. Bad. Bad."

Right now, I feel bad. Like even though Meghan did a lot of bad things to me, was it wrong of me to do something bad back? *Yes? No? Maybe?!?*

I pull the covers up over my head to block out the answer.

Thinking isn't going to help me feel better. Neither is turning on my phone. Leaving it off means I won't have to read the comments on my post. It's a stall tactic. But a good one.

So is getting to school as late as possible.

Slowly, I get out of bed and take my time getting dressed. White jeans. Purple top. Red sneaks. Then I change. Black leggings. Pink cardigan. Gray ballet flats. I take my time French braiding my hair into two long pigtails.

When I'm finished, I put the copy of my speech that I printed out for Mrs. Lee's approval and my phone into my backpack and head to the kitchen to make breakfast—the kind that takes as long as possible to make. I crack eggs into a pan and put bread in the toaster. I pour myself a glass of juice.

Sooner than I'd like, I'm in the car on the way to school with Mom and Dad, who still haven't gotten back to me about the verdict on Capitol-gate (my word, not theirs). And I haven't exactly thought up a brilliant solution for how to persuade Mom to do the tour.

But that's a problem I'll have to deal with tonight. Now, I need to see if I have another one. Stalling is no longer an option. Better to know what I'm dealing with before I get to school.

Reluctantly, I turn on my phone and see dozens of missed calls and text messages. All from Ben.

> Ben: ADAMS! What have you done?

> Ben: Hey Adams! U There???

> Ben: Alive

> Ben: Where R U?

> Ben: Call me.

> Ben: NOW!!

> Ben: 911! Get here quick!

> Ben: OMG!

> Ben: It's bad.

> Ben: Real bad!

My stomach goes into free fall as I imagine Ben's definition of bad. I see angry faces. Especially Meghan's. Pitchforks. Principal Ferguson with a trash bag that has my name on it. As Dad pulls into the drop-off lane, I don't even have to wonder what awaits me at school. There's Ben. One look at his grim expression is all I need to know that whatever happened is serious.

"Adams, where've you been?" he asks.

"Sorry, my phone was off."

Ben rolls his eyes like that's no excuse. "Seriously, what did you do last night?"

Heat creeps up the back of my neck. I know Ben isn't talking about the time I spent putting the finishing touches on my speech. He means the Instagram post.

"Adams, everyone is talking about how you sold out Meghan and spilled the beans on her crush. That was low. I would have told you not to do it." He shoots me a look. "Remember the burrito thing?"

"Yeah," I mumble.

"Like, what happened to making all decisions together? I thought you were going to finish your speech and find a way to persuade your mom to give us the tour."

"I finished the speech. The other thing is still a work in progress. I can't undo what I did," I say. A bunch of kids in our grade are shooting us looks, and something tells me things are worse than Ben is saying. "I'm sorry. I know it was wrong. I should have talked to you first. But Meghan called me a liar and I snapped."

"Got it," Ben says. "Not smart. But stuff happens." He pauses. "Adams, there's something else you need to know."

"Spit it out," I say, even though I'm a ten on the *dreading-what-he-has-to-say* scale.

"A picture is worth a thousand words." Ben leads me down the hall to the bulletin board near Mrs. Lee's room. On it is my campaign poster. Only now, there's a mustache and a goatee drawn on my face with #LIAR written across it. "All our posters look like that," he says.

My mouth falls open, but no words come out. It was bad enough that Meghan called me a liar and that I spilled her secret. *But this?* I can't believe what I'm seeing.

I hear whispers behind me. Then voices. And one in particular that I recognize. I whirl around to face my former best friend and the candidate who I'm sure defaced my poster.

I point to it. "Did you do this?" I hiss at Meghan.

She doesn't answer the question. She says, "The truth hurts, doesn't it?"

"Who's the liar?" I narrow my eyes at Meghan. "Seriously? How could you do this to my posters? It's like something a little kid would do to another kid's drawings. Not what seventh graders do to an opponent's campaign posters."

Meghan's mouth snaps open, then shut, like she's not sure what to say.

But I am. "I can't believe you would ruin my posters."

"Look, I didn't do this," Meghan says under her breath.

A list of all of Meghan's wrongs, from the moment she told me she was running against me, plays like a loop in my head. "You started this," I hiss at her. "By running against me."

Meghan's hands are on her hips like she has the right to be mad. "Anyone can run for president," Meghan hisses back. "And I'm not the one who spilled secrets. You did!"

"You called me a liar," I remind her.

"Catfight!" someone yells. I ignore the whistles and voices

around me. The only thing I'm focused on is Meghan as we exchange words I never thought we'd be saying to each other. Especially at school. As our voices grow louder, the ones behind me seem to fade.

"I'll never forgive you. Ever." Meghan spits her words at me and moves closer.

I don't care if she does. "I'll never forgive you, either," I spit back, my face inches from hers like we're both contemplating fighting each other. Then someone is pulling us apart.

It's Mrs. Lee. "Girls!" she barks, her voice harsher than I've ever heard it. We both look up at her shaking her head at us. "I couldn't be any more disappointed in either of you."

Then she marches us straight to Principal Ferguson's office.

Chapter Twenty-One
"PLUS ÇA CHANGE, PLUS ÇA RESTE"
(IN ENGLISH: "THE MORE THINGS CHANGE, THE MORE THEY STAY THE SAME")

Nasty posts. Name-calling. Ruined posters." Principal Ferguson's arms are wrapped tightly around the width of his chest. "Frankly, I'm shocked by what Mrs. Lee told me. And to think that you're supposed to be friends." He makes a loud *tssk* sound.

Meghan and I both open our mouths to speak, but Principal Ferguson motions for us to stay silent. "You'll have your chance to talk. But not yet. And not to me."

Meghan and I glare at each other. If we're not going to be talking to our principal, who will we be talking to? Our parents? The honor board? The police!?!

Principal Ferguson steps from behind his desk, then

motions for Meghan and me to follow him to a small storage room next to his office. It reeks of the musty smell of stacks of old textbooks that line the walls. In the middle of the room is a small table and two chairs. "Ladies, you've allowed this election to turn into a nasty competition between friends, setting a terrible example for the students you will potentially be leading. I'm disappointed. Mrs. Lee is disappointed. I've spoken to your parents, and they couldn't be any more disappointed."

Principal Ferguson shoots me an *especially yours* look, and the hot flush of shame creeps up the back of my neck. I can hear the lecture I'm going to get from Mom and Dad about how they didn't raise a daughter to run a nasty campaign. How they expected more. But I don't have time to contemplate what they're going to say, because Principal Ferguson keeps talking.

"My idea of a punishment was to disqualify you both from the election. But Mrs. Lee had an idea we both agree is more fitting."

Meghan and I exchange a look like neither of us likes the sound of that.

Principal Ferguson points to the two chairs. "Have a seat. You'll be spending the morning here. Just the two of you. I expect you to work out your differences. I also expect each one of you to come up with a new speech—one that unifies the grade, not tears it apart. Mrs. Lee and I both look forward to reading your thoughts on how that can be done."

He straightens his tie before finishing. "We'll be back at

lunchtime. Think of this as a test you both have to pass. If you both do, you can give your speeches to your whole grade tomorrow. And if either of you fails, you can both congratulate Frankie Chang on becoming the new president of the seventh grade. Good luck. I suggest you work together." Mr. Ferguson shuts the door behind him as he leaves.

Meghan and I huff. Then glare at each other. It's just the two of us for the next three and a half hours. Not where I want to be. I'm pretty sure by the icy stares coming my way that it's not where she wants to be, either.

The clock on the wall ticks loudly as it creeps forward, but Meghan's mouth stays clamped shut and so does mine.

So much has happened since this campaign started that it's hard to know where to begin.

Tick tock. Tick tock. Tick tock. Meghan and I just sit staring at each other. Then a realization hits me: time is wasting. And if Meghan and I don't work together to use what remains of our morning, we can both kiss this election goodbye.

Finally, I'm the one to break the silence. I roll my eyes at our surroundings. "We got put into the isolation cabin like the Parker sisters in *The Parent Trap*." I wait, unsure what Meghan's reaction will be. But she gives me a small smile when I reference our all-time favorite movie.

"Yeah," she says. "Not much different from where we started in first grade."

I can't help but smile at the memory of Mrs. Hudson putting us in time-out on our first day of first grade at Patriot Elementary. "We messed up, didn't we? Again?"

"Big time," says Meghan. Her eyes flicker with an emotion I haven't seen for a while.

"Meghan, I'm really—"

But before the word *sorry* comes out of my mouth, Meghan cuts me off. "Amanda, I'm the one who's sorry. I should have told you I was going to run against you. But all you talked about before the election was how you wanted to be president." She shrugs. "I was mad at you."

I get that. And I'm not proud of it. "I'm sorry if I was being selfish," I say, then I add the thing that's been on my mind since this campaign started. "I just wish you had told me you wanted to run, too."

Meghan looks down for several seconds, then back up at me. "There's something you need to know," she finally says. "It was Bree's idea for me to run against you and for her to be my vice president."

Confusion swirls around me. I don't get it. "Why didn't she just run for president?" I ask.

Meghan bites her lip before responding. "She didn't want to be president. Too much work. And she thought it would be funny if two best friends ran against each other."

"Funny?" I ask, not sure how that's funny.

"I know. It was wrong. I think she just meant that everyone would be into an election with one best friend running against another."

My nose wrinkles. "I don't like the idea that Bree thought you versus me would be good entertainment, but I get it. I guess what I don't get is why you went along with it."

Meghan pauses before answering. When she starts to speak, her voice cracks, like she's trying not to cry. "Amanda, I feel awful about what I'm going to say. But when Bree told me she wanted to be friends, I went along with her plan because I wanted to be friends with her, too. I'm embarrassed to admit this, but she's so popular, and I was just kind of surprised and happy she wanted to be friends with me." Meghan shrugs. "Stupid. I know."

I stare down at a fuzz ball on my cardigan. "Wow," I mumble, unsure what else to say. My lifelong best friend dumped me for cool, pretty, popular Bree Simon.

"Amanda." Meghan says my name, and I look up to see tears pooling in her eyes. "I'm so sorry. It was mean. And stupid. Now that I've gotten to know Bree, I'm not even sure I like her."

I listen quietly while Meghan elaborates. "After the interview, I told Bree that I knew by the way you were tapping your foot when you were answering Stella's questions, you hadn't even asked your mom about taking us on the field trip," she says.

Meghan gives me a tentative smile. "Don't forget, we've been best friends for a long time, and I know you tap your foot only when you're lying." She pauses, then adds, "It was Bree's idea for me to do the liar post. And she was the one who drew on your posters. But I didn't stop her . . . and I should have."

I blow out a breath. On one hand, it's kind of cool to think that Meghan knows me well enough to know when I'm making something up. But on the other hand, it hurts to think she went along with Bree just because she wanted to be her friend.

"Amanda, I know I shouldn't have done what I did. It was really wrong, and I'm sorry."

Now, tears are rolling down Meghan's cheeks, and she wipes her nose on the sleeve of her new white sweater. It leaves a gross wet spot, but Meghan doesn't seem to mind.

This makes me get teary-eyed. Not rolling-down-my-cheeks tears. Just the kind that roll slowly from the corners of my eyes and make me realize how much I've missed my best friend. What Meghan did was wrong. But she wasn't the only one who did something wrong.

"I'm sorry, too," I whisper, even though we're the only ones in this little room. "I feel awful that I told everyone about your secret crush."

Meghan's face is the color of a red apple. "Umm, yeah. That was bad."

"I know," I say. "I wish I could undo what I did."

"Me too," says Meghan. "I wish we could undo everything we both did."

"We're boneheads," I add.

Meghan giggles, then gives me a hopeful look. "Think we can go back to being besties?"

I don't have to stop to think about my answer. "Yeah," I say. "I'd like that." Meghan and I did bad things to each other. But I'll always love Meghan and want her to be my best friend. Hopefully she'll always feel the same way about me.

Meghan holds out her right pinky in my direction. "Let's pinky swear that nothing—not an election or another person or anything—will ever come between us. EVER!"

I repeat the word. "EVER!"

Meghan and I pinky swear and hug. We sit there for a minute, in happy silence. But then we both realize that the only sound in the room is the clock ticking on the wall. We've used up almost an hour, and there are other things we need to be doing. AND FAST! Before Mrs. Lee and Principal Ferguson return.

My eyes focus on Meghan. "Um, Meghan," I say, "if either one of us is going to win this election, we've got a lot to do and not much time to do it."

"Yeah," she says. "We're not giving this to Frankie Chang."

"No way," I say. Meghan and I have our differences, but we have one thing in common: we both like to win. And even though we both know two candidates can't win one election, neither will win if we don't figure out a way to work together.

So Meghan and I get to it.

✳ ✳ ✳

MY CAMPAIGN INSPIRATION NOTEBOOK

- - - - - - - - - -

✳ Barack Obama ✳

BORN: August 4, 1961, in Hawaii

SIGN: Leo. Traits: Inspiring, optimistic, humorous. Known for believing the world is a stage.

PARTY: Democrat

STATUS: Married to Michelle

KIDS: Sasha and Malia

PRESIDENCY: He became the 44th president of our nation in 2008

NICKNAME: No Drama Obama, because he ran a campaign that didn't have much of it. And because he was known as being super chill, patient, and relaxed.

PETS: Bo and Sunny, Portuguese water dogs

SIDE GIGS: Makes good chili, and loves sports and his dogs!

FAMOUS SPEECH: His 2004 speech at the Democratic National Convention

IMPORTANT FIRSTS: First African American president

✳ ✳ ✳

The campaign for president of my class officially ends tomorrow, Speech Day. And the speech I'm going to make is totally different from the speech I thought I would be making. But here's the good news: Mrs. Lee liked it a lot. So did Principal Ferguson. Best of all, Mom and Dad did, too. Which was a VERY, VERY good thing! Because my parents were really mad (like a ten thousand on the mad scale) at me about what happened.

But when they heard how Meghan and I resolved things and what I have planned for my speech tomorrow, they got a whole lot less mad. Not un-mad. They still banned me from all social media for a month. But they both said they believe I learned an important campaign lesson: That no elected position is worth having if you have to fight dirty to get it.

Then Dad reminded me that I still needed to kill tomorrow's speech. To do that, he suggested I read up on our nation's forty-fourth president, Barack Obama, who, he said, will be remembered as one of the greatest speakers of all time.

So here goes.

What is it that made President Obama soooooo good at speaking?

One: President Obama knew what to say and when to say it.

Even more important, how to say it. President Obama spoke slowly when he wanted people to remember what he had to say and sped up when he had a lot to say that people might not want to spend much time listening to. Personally, I think that is something teachers at Liberty Middle School were not taught to do. Especially Mr. Corbett, who always takes his sweet time explaining algebraic equations like they're something that the students in his first-period class actually want to hear about.

Not the point.

Bottom line: Keep your audience awake.

Two: President Obama had a lot of style.

He had a good sense of humor. He knew that people like a good laugh. (I bet President Obama and Ben would get along great.)

President Obama's voice was loud, strong, and clear. Dad has always said that if you have something to say, say it like you mean it. Obama nailed that.

President Obama used hand gestures to make a point. I've never thought about it before, but according to my research, confident speakers use a lot of hand gestures when they speak.

And when President Obama had something super important to say, he repeated it. Not in an annoying way. But in a way that let his audience know it was important to him, and he wanted whatever it was he was talking about to be important to them, too.

Bottom line: Tomorrow when I make my speech, I need to be funny. Speak loudly and clearly. Throw in a few hand gestures. And repeat the important stuff.

Um. Yeah. That's a lot to remember. All I can do is my best. Moving on.

Three: President Obama had something important to say.

Dad told me I should look up the speech he made at the 2004 Democratic National Convention as an example of a speech with an important message. It was about bringing together a divided nation. So I looked it up. Here are the most famous words from Obama's speech:

"There's not a liberal America and a conservative America; there's the United States of America. There's not a black America and white America and Latino America and Asian America; there's the United States of America."

I know the message Dad wanted me to get here is that words can heal. Tomorrow, mine need to. Another thing that's cool about Obama's words (besides the words themselves) is that he wrote them himself. One thing I've learned in my research about past presidents is that they all had speech writers. Obama did too. Sometimes he used them. And sometimes he didn't, like when he wrote this speech.

Obama had something important to say, and he said it.

> **Bottom line: I have something important I need to say, too. I'm nervous, but I'm also excited to say it.**

Four: President Obama believed in his message.

Obama's speech writers referred to his 2004 speech about one United States of America as "Obama's love letter to

America." After that, whenever they wrote speeches for him, that's the speech they would use for guidance. Obama was emotional about his message. He believed in what he was saying. He spoke from his heart and found his way into the hearts of the people.

If I want to win this election, that's exactly what I need to do, too.

Chapter Twenty-Two

AMANDA'S "LOVE LETTER" TO THE SEVENTH GRADE OF LIBERTY MIDDLE SCHOOL

I shift in my chair and glance at the other presidential candidates and vice presidential candidates seated alongside me on the auditorium stage. Then I look out at the sea of seventh-grade faces in the audience. Some look like they're paying attention. Others look like they're bored out of their minds. A few are asleep.

I refocus on the task at hand. My classmates have already heard two candidates speak. Yesterday, Principal Ferguson decided the fairest way to determine the order of speakers was to choose names out of a hat. So Frankie went first. He was introduced by Annalise. Then Bree introduced Meghan and she spoke. Now it's Ben's turn to introduce me.

I give him a good-luck nod as he walks to the podium.

Ben taps the microphone and the sound of his fingers drumming against it echoes loudly. Several of the sleeping kids jolt upright. Not a bad start. I'd like everyone to be awake to hear what I have to say. Ben leans over the microphone and begins.

"What would you get if you crossed a gorilla with the sixteenth U.S. President?" He doesn't wait before delivering the punch line. "Ape Lincoln."

There are a few giggles, but mostly groans. I see Mom and Dad, who came to hear me give my speech, exchange a look. I send a no-more-jokes signal from my brain to Ben's. Fortunately, he seems to get it. His post-joke grin disappears and his face turns serious.

"I'm Ben Ball, hopefully your next vice president, and I have an important job this morning," he says. "I get to introduce our third and final candidate for president of our class."

He turns and looks at me, then speaks loudly and clearly into the microphone. "I'm proud to introduce Amanda Adams, my pick for president. And after you hear what she has to say, I feel confident she'll be yours, too. Give it up for Amanda."

There's *some* clapping. On the audience reaction scale, it's a five, which makes my nerves shoot straight to ten. Frankie got about the same amount of applause after he spoke. But Meghan got more like a seven or eight.

I step up to the podium and my eyes settle on Dad. He gives me a nod.

I straighten my shoulders and begin. "I want to start this morning by congratulating my fellow candidates, who did a really good job speaking. And trust me," I say, my voice shakier than I want it to be, "standing up in front of all of you and speaking is harder than it looks."

I take a deep breath. "My opponents have lots of good ideas, really good ideas," I say, gathering my courage. "One of the things I learned in this election is that a leader needs to be a good listener. That means recognizing when someone else has a good idea, and sometimes an idea that is better than your own. Both of my opponents have some of those."

I turn around and gesture to Frankie. "I agree with Frankie that we all could use an extra study hall to get more of our homework done in school. If I'm elected, I'll definitely talk to the school administration about that. And if Frankie is elected, I'll help him try to get it done."

I think about Obama's sense of humor and take a chance at interjecting some of my own here. "And if we can't get an additional study hall, I'll talk to the teachers about less homework."

There's laughter. Then applause from the audience. This

time it's a six on the enthusiastic response scale, and I feel myself starting to relax behind the podium.

I turn around again, and this time I look at Meghan. She smiles at me. Meghan was the first one to read what's in my speech, so she knows what's coming next.

And she likes it.

"I also think Meghan's idea of cleaning up Sandy Point State Park and then having a beach party sounds like a lot of fun. If I'm elected, I'm going to appoint Meghan Hart to be on the planning committee to make sure it happens. And if she's elected, I'm going to volunteer to be on her committee."

"Beachbound!" someone yells.

There's more applause. It's a seven. Or maybe an eight. It's pretty clear everyone likes the idea of a beach cleanup and party. Me too.

I clear my throat. The next part of my speech is the most important part. And also the hardest to say. "A lot of bad things happened during the campaign. I was responsible for some of those things. I'm not proud of my actions, but if I want to be a leader of my class, I know that I have to own what I did and vow to do better."

Just like Obama, I deliver the next part of my speech loudly and clearly, emphasizing the importance of my words. "I want to apologize to my fellow candidates whom I wronged. I want to apologize to my classmates for not setting a better example.

As well as to the administration of our school for any trouble I caused, especially to Principal Ferguson and Mrs. Lee."

I look at Mrs. Lee, who gives me a thumbs-up, and I'm filled with an overwhelming sense of relief. Whatever happens in this election, I know my favorite teacher feels like I'm finally doing my best as a candidate for president of my class. Best of all, I know I am too.

I glance down at the sheet of paper in front of me, but I don't need to read from it. Not when the rest of what I'm about to say comes straight from my heart.

"I also want to apologize to my parents, especially my mom. I made a promise that if I won this election, my mom would take our class on a tour of the Capitol. I'm ashamed to admit this, but she never promised to do that."

There's a loud gasp from the audience. Kids are twisting in their seats to look at my mom, who's sitting in the middle of the auditorium next to Meghan's mom and Frankie's parents.

I wait for the crowd to quiet before I continue.

"I've learned that one of the most important rules of any campaign is to never promise something you can't deliver." I pause, then add, "Trust me, I got in a lot of trouble for doing that. I've learned my lesson and can honestly promise I'll never do that again. But the good news is that I figured out a way to make the tour happen."

There are whispers and more gasps. Now, lots of kids are

looking at Mom. Not just like they think it's cool that there's a United States congresswoman in the house, but also like they're curious about what I did to persuade her to go along with my plan. So I tell them.

"When I told my mom what I'd promised, she said that she couldn't take our class on a Capitol tour because it wasn't fair to all of the other seventh grades that she represents. So I thought long and hard about that." I pause, then add, "She was right. An elected official, whether he or she is the congressperson of a state or the president of a grade, must represent *all* of the people, not just *some* of the people. And that gave me an idea."

I smile at Mom and she gives me a smile back, like she approves of what I'm about to say.

"During the campaign, my parents made me keep a notebook about past presidents of the United States. At first, I didn't want to do it. I didn't see how it would help me get elected. Our nation's leaders didn't always do the right thing, but I learned a lot about being a leader. I learned a lot, from presidents like George Washington, Thomas Jefferson, Abraham Lincoln, Theodore Roosevelt, Franklin Delano Roosevelt, John F. Kennedy, Richard Nixon, and Barack Obama."

My voice is loud and clear as I deliver the next part of my speech. "But I learned even more about what it means to be a leader by running for president myself. And it made me realize that other students at other schools will learn a lot if they run, too. So I suggested to my mom that she start an essay writing contest about what it means to be a leader."

I wait a beat before I tell everyone about the details of the contest.

"All students in my mom's district who run in middle school elections can enter. Every year, she'll pick a winner and give the winner's whole grade a tour of the Capitol. My mom loved the idea, and said that our class will have the first winner. So no matter who wins this election, whether it's Frankie, or Meghan, or me, my mom agreed to take our whole grade on a tour of the Capitol."

Every student in the auditorium starts clapping and cheering like crazy, and it doesn't stop until Principal Ferguson stands and holds up his arm. When the auditorium is quiet again, he motions for me to finish my speech.

"In closing, I just want to say that we're all on the same team, with one goal—to make our school the very best it can be. During this election process, I've made new friends. Despite some of my actions, I've also managed to keep the old friends. Most important, I believe I've learned a lot about what it means to be a leader, and I promise that if you vote for me for president of the seventh grade, I will do my best each and every day to be the best president ever. Thank you."

I hold my breath while everyone claps and cheers.

Finally, I exhale, relieved, because on the audience reaction scale, it's a ten.

Chapter Twenty-Three

PARTY LIKE A ROCK STAR. OR A SEVENTH-GRADE CLASS PRESIDENT!

WOO HOO! I, Amanda Elizabeth Adams, am officially (as of 12:17 p.m. today, when Principal Ferguson called Frankie, Annalise, Meghan, Bree, Ben, and me to his office to tell us the outcome of the election) the new president of the seventh grade at Liberty Middle School.

It still feels surreal that I won.

Before Principal Ferguson announced the results, he gave us all a speech about how the campaign had some low moments. But that it all worked out in the end. And he said that no matter the outcome, he wanted us all to stay involved and work as class leaders. Then he looked at me and said the magic words.

"Congratulations, Amanda. You're president."

What happened next was a blur. Meghan hugged me. Frankie shook my hand. Ben was high-fiving me. And everyone (especially Meghan) was saying things like: *"You gave a really great speech"* and *"You're going to make an awesome president."*

The rest of the school day, kids in my class and all of my teachers congratulated me.

When the last bell rang, Mom and Dad were waiting to take me home. I think Mr. Ferguson must have tipped them off. They were in the pick-up line and looked happier than two little kids with plastic pumpkins full of candy on Halloween.

Mom was first to hug me. "No election victory is sweeter than your first one," she said.

Dad ruffled my hair, and then he gave me a hug, too.

"We're so proud of you!" gushed Mom once we were all in the car. "And I'm still impressed that you managed to think of such a smart way to spin the Capitol tour." She flashed my dad a loving look. "She's a chip off her father's strategist block," Mom added.

"And her mother's candidate block," said Dad.

Then he turned around and smiled at me. "Amanda, I know it was a tough campaign. They all are." He paused for a moment before putting the car into gear. "I'm proud to have another winning candidate in the family."

"Thanks," I said. "For all of your support."

Then Mom added, "Amanda, this was a wonderful learning experience for you. And you'll be even better prepared for your next campaign."

At that point, I burst out laughing. I couldn't help it. Mom is one of those people who is always 100 percent focused on what's next. "Mom, I just won this election. I'm happy to be president of the seventh grade. I have no idea if I have any future political aspirations."

"Just be the best president you can be," she said. "And I know you will."

- - - - - - - - - -

It takes effort, but when my phone buzzes in my hand, I open my eyes. I can't believe I actually fell asleep when I got home from school. But then again, it's not so surprising. I was so nervous about giving a speech. Then waiting all morning to find out who won the election.

I sit up on my bed and read the incoming text message. It's from Meghan.

> Meghan: What are you wearing to your victory party?!?

> Amanda: IDK. Help!

> Meghan: Yellow smiley face sweatshirt!

Amanda: ☺ 👍

Meghan: Congrats again!

Meghan: Can't wait to celebrate with you. 🎉👀

Amanda: C U soon!

I get up and pull on my sweatshirt, then brush my hair and wind it into two neat braids. Just as I'm finishing, I hear the doorbell ring. When I open the door, Ben grins at me.

"PARTY TIME!" he shouts. Then he heads straight to my dining room. Minutes later, it is filled with everyone who wants to celebrate our victory—the kids who voted for us, the kids who heard Ben was giving out more burrito and smoothie coupons, Meghan, and even Bree, who apologized for ruining my posters and volunteered to help out on whatever committee I need her on. Best of all, the girls from my soccer team are all there.

In the end, it wasn't even my speech (though they all said it was great) that swayed them to vote for me. It was the fact that we're a team, and team members stick together through the good and the bad. But they did make me promise not to take my eyes off the ball at the next game.

I made that promise, and it's one I plan to keep!

Ben taps me on the shoulder and I look into his huge grin. "Hey, Adams, your dad sure knows how to put on a party," he says.

I smile and survey the dining room table. It's covered with

Papa Rocco's pizza, soda, and bowls of Skittles and M&Ms. Ben is right. Dad did pull together a killer party. He's put on enough victory parties for Mom to know how to do it right. Ben taps a knife against a soda bottle, and the room goes quiet. "I think everyone is waiting for the victor to make a speech," he says.

"Speech!" some of the girls on the soccer team chorus together.

I clear my throat. "I'm going to keep this short. You've all listened to me talk, like, waaaaay too much today." The room fills with laughs, and I keep going. "I just want to say that I'm really excited to be president. I'm going to do my best to do a good job. I want to thank all of you for being here and supporting me. Especially Ben."

I look at him and he blushes, something I didn't know Ben Ball was capable of doing.

"Ben, I couldn't have done this without you." I pause, then add, "It's funny how things work out. If you'd told me at the beginning of this campaign that you would end up being my vice president, let alone my good friend, I might have laughed. But the more I got to know you, the more I realized just how funny and nice you are. So seriously, thanks for everything. For all your help. But most of all for being my friend." I flash Ben a huge smile. "And I know you're going to make a great veep!"

He smiles back at me, then bows and says, "At your service, Madame President." And the whole room cracks up.

"Okay, that's it for the speech. Eat. Have fun!" I shout above the laughter and noise.

And everyone does.

I listen to the happy sounds of the victory party going on around me, and I exhale.

It's crazy to think that I won, especially after everything that happened. And even crazier to think that I won because of my speech. I guess in the end, donuts and big signs and fancy stickers and even cool ideas about things like extra time in school to do homework and beach parties aren't what it takes to win an election.

I think it was honesty and integrity that pushed my campaign over the edge.

And who knows . . . maybe free burritos and smoothies helped, too.

Chapter Twenty-Four

ON THE SLEEPOVER SCALE, THIS ONE'S A TEN

I tuck one of the throw pillows from Meghan's bed under my head, then stuff a potato chip in my mouth while I wait for Meghan to tell me the BIG news she's been saving.

"Okay. Okay," says Meghan. "But this is big."

"Um, the last time you had big news—"

Meghan laughs. She knows I'm just teasing her. "Drumroll, please."

I slap my palms against my thighs.

Meghan clears her throat. "I have a boyfriend!"

"Holy guacamole! Caleb?"

Meghan grins. "None other."

We squeal together, long and loud, then Meghan tells me the whole story.

"When he found out I had a crush on him, he told me that he's had one on me, too, but that he was too shy to tell me."

"Caleb J? Shy?" On the surprised scale, I'm a ten. I mean, who would have thought that the star quarterback of the football team would be scared to tell a girl he liked her?"

Meghan nodded. "I was surprised, too. But he's really shy. And sweet." Meghan nibbles a chip. "Caleb told me he's had a crush on me since he was in fourth grade and I was in third at Patriot. He used to see me playing on the monkey bars and knew I was the girl for him."

"No way!" A memory of those monkey bars on the playground at our elementary school makes me smile. Meghan and I used to climb on them every day at recess.

"Yeah," says Meghan. She pulls a little gold heart on a chain from underneath the collar of her T-shirt and holds it out for me to see. "He gave me this necklace last night and asked me if I wanted to be his girlfriend. And I said yes!"

This time when we squeal it's even louder than we were when Meghan's dad bought us tickets in sixth grade to go to the Jingle Ball, where Shawn Mendes was performing.

"I wanted you to know first," Meghan says, "since you're my best friend." Meghan pauses. "And I want to thank you for spilling the beans."

"Um, about that . . ." A fresh wave of guilt washes over me.

"Don't worry," says Meghan. "If you hadn't told my secret, Caleb would never have known I liked him, and he never would have told me he likes me. So, it's cool. Everything worked out the way it was supposed to."

"Wow!" I say. It's pretty incredible that Meghan has her first boyfriend. And even more incredible to think that something good came out of me doing something bad. Like telling my best friend's secret. *Ugh.* I still can't believe I did that. I give Meghan a serious look. "I'm glad it all worked out, but I promise I'll never tell one of your secrets again."

"I know you won't." Meghan sighs. "I'm really sorry, Amanda, about everything that happened."

"Yeah. Me too," I say. "Winning the election was important. But keeping you as my best friend is even more important." My words sound kind of corny, but I need Meghan to know how I feel. "From now on, I'm going to be even better than a best friend. I'm going to be the most amazing best friend ever."

"That makes two of us," says Meghan.

Our eyes meet and I tell her what I've been holding in since I arrived. "Um, I have some news of my own. Drumroll, please!"

Now it's Meghan's turn to slap her palms against her thighs.

"I'm getting something I've always wanted."

Meghan's nose wrinkles. "Highlights?"

I roll my eyes. Meghan knows neither of my parents would

ever say yes to that. I clear my throat. "Mom finally said yes . . . to me getting a dog!"

Meghan reaches over to hug me, then starts firing questions, about when and where I'm getting a dog and what kind of dog I'm getting, faster than I can answer them.

"Tomorrow, Mom and Dad are taking me to the shelter to pick one out. And I want you to come with me to help. Will you?"

"Yes!" squeals Meghan. "Yes! Yes! Yes! Yes! Yes! But wait, what made your mom change her mind?"

"That's a whole other story." Then I tell it to Meghan.

I smile. Which is impossible not to do when I've got one dog in my lap and another one licking my face. "They're both so cute. I don't know how I'll choose. Can I have two?" I ask.

"NO!" Mom and Dad say at the same time.

Picking one dog from all the ones at the shelter is a nearly impossible task. If Meghan hadn't come with me today, I don't know how I would have even narrowed it down to the final two. But now I have to choose between a little fluffy white dog named Fifi or a big brown-and-white spotted dog named George, who can't seem to stop licking me.

"Amanda, the spotted dog is cute," says Mom. "And I like his name."

I look at Meghan and we both crack up. My best friend knows

as well as I do that my mom has never had an opinion on what makes for a cute dog name. It's pretty obvious she likes him because he shares a name with our nation's first president—nice publicity for a congresswoman who is about to be photographed adopting a dog with her daughter at the local shelter.

In case you're wondering, that's why Mom finally agreed to the idea of me getting a dog. Good photo op. And I told her the story about Nixon and how Checkers saved his career. Not that hers needs saving. The point being, a dog can do wonders for a politician.

"It's all about using the media to your advantage," I told Mom.

When I said that, Mom was hooked. "If I can make my daughter happy and score some political points, then why not," she said to Dad, who agreed wholeheartedly.

I smile to myself. It's cool that my original campaign idea to get a dog worked after all.

Dad winks at me like he knows what I'm thinking. To be honest, I think Dad is just as excited about this dog as I am.

I rub the fur behind George's floppy ears and he lays his big head on my shoulder. I grin.

"I think I found my dog," I say.

George licks my face (again!) like he approves of the idea. And just like that, I'm the one who's hooked.

Chapter Twenty-Five
AN INSIDER'S VIEW
(OR, MY MOM HAS HER MOMENTS)

Kind of hard to believe I'm standing here—which happens to be in the Rotunda of the United States Capitol—with everyone else in my grade, and my mom is our personal tour guide. It's like Take Your Daughter to Work Day, except in this case, it's take her and her whole class.

Mom gestures to the large dome above us and every eye of every student (plus the chaperones, which include Mrs. Lee and Coach Newton) looks straight up. One hundred eighty feet up, to be exact. Mom just told us that that's the height of the Rotunda (which also happens to be ninety-six feet wide).

On the big scale, this rotunda is a ten.

Everyone listens without saying a word (something that almost never happens at Liberty Middle School) as Mom explains the history of the art on the Rotunda canopy and how it was painted in 1865 by an artist named Constantino Brumidi.

"It took him almost one full year to paint it," Mom says.

"It's awesome," Meghan whispers into my ear.

I nod. It really is amazing. I've seen it before, with Mom, but I get chills all over again just looking up at it and imagining how hard it must have been for the artist to paint it.

"The Rotunda is used for important events, like inaugurations and presidential funerals," Mom says. Then she tells my whole grade all kinds of cool facts about the history of the artwork on the walls and about many of the busts and statues around the Rotunda.

After that, we go to see the National Statuary Hall, which has sculptures that represent many of the states. Even though Mom is a congresswoman for just one of those states, she knows a lot about the history of many of the others, too.

"It's way cool how much your mom knows about this place," Ben says to me.

"Yeah," I say. It is cool. And surprising. I had no clue Mom knew so much about art. Nice to think you can be surprised by your mom . . . in good ways!

When we're done in the Statuary Hall, Mom leads us through the Crypt. The name of it sounds spooky—like something straight out of a horror movie—but it's not that at all. It's a room filled with forty beautiful brown stone columns that support the floor of the Rotunda above and thirteen marble sculptures that represent the original colonies.

"This is where George Washington was supposed to be buried," Mom says in her tour-guide voice. "But he stipulated in his will that he wanted to be buried at Mount Vernon."

Mom motions for our group to keep walking. She talks as she walks, filling everyone in on all kinds of cool trivia about the Capitol. It has 540 rooms and 658 windows. Underground tunnels and a private subway connect the main building of the Capitol with all of the congressional office buildings.

"All the rooms in the Capitol are designated as either *S* for *Senate* or *H* for *House* depending on whether they are in the north wing, where the Senate members have their offices, or in the south wing, where the House members have theirs," Mom says. Then she adds that there are marble bathtubs in the basement of the Capitol, where members of Congress would take baths in the nineteenth century.

Meghan giggles. "Ew! Gross!"

I try not to crack up. But I can't help it. It's pretty weird to think about all those lawmakers way back when taking their bubble baths at work. "Think they had little yellow rubber duckies that floated around in the marble tubs?" I ask.

Meghan and I are giggling like crazy about the idea of all those old lawmakers splish-splashing around with their rubber duckies, until a hand taps us on our shoulders.

"Ladies, care to share what's so amusing?"

Meghan and I snap out of our giggle fit and look into the face of Mrs. Lee. But it's obvious by the look on her face that she's not really mad. So I tell her why we're laughing.

"Ah, I see what you mean," she says, like she sees the humor of it, too.

Mom leads our group to the last stop on our tour—The House Galleries, where visitors can watch the United States House of Representatives in action. They're not in session today, but Mom paints a picture (with words, not a paintbrush) of what it's like when they're legislating.

"The elected officials of this country have an important job," she says. "And it's one that my coworkers in both the House and the Senate take very seriously."

I listen proudly while Mom talks about what lawmakers do and how laws in our country are made. "Bottom line, it's the job of your elected officials to make our country a better place," Mom says. "But it's also the job of every citizen of this nation to do their part by getting involved. If you believe in something, take a stand. Be a part of what you want to see changed."

As I look down at the big room of seats that are usually filled with representatives from all fifty states, it amazes me to think that my mom is one of them. Her job is an important one. I know how hard it was to get elected president of the seventh grade; it really must have taken a lot of hard work to get where she is.

And it inspires me. That sounds corny, but it's true. Mom is doing her part to make our nation a better place. And it makes me really excited to do my part at my school.

Mom asks if anyone has questions, then patiently answers them. When she's finished, Mrs. Lee presents my mom with a special plaque.

"This was an amazing tour, and we can't thank you enough," she says.

When the tour ends, I zip through the crowd straight to Mom.

"That was awesome!" I give Mom a tight squeeze, even though I know she doesn't like me to do that when she's dressed in her work clothes. But today, she squeezes me right back.

"Mom, you've surprised me a lot lately. All in good ways," I say.

Not only did she agree to this tour, but she let me get a dog, and she was there for me through the whole campaign and all of the drama with Meghan, even though she's really busy with her own work.

I flash her a grateful smile. "Seriously, Mom, thanks."

Mom wraps an arm around my shoulder. "Mom first. Congresswoman second," she whispers into my ear, then plants a big kiss right on the top of my head.

Chapter Twenty-Six

WHY IS THIS SOCCER GAME DIFFERENT FROM ALL OTHER SOCCER GAMES? OR AT LEAST THE LAST ONE AGAINST BROOKSIDE?

A ball hurtles toward me and I kick it back in the direction it came from. A chorus of cheers goes up in the stands, but I don't take my eyes off the field. I'm too focused on the game to care about cheering. Or anything else, for that matter.

Right now, the only thing on my mind is beating Revere, and we're on our way to doing it. The score is 3–0 with less than two minutes to go in the second half. And if I have anything to do with it, Revere won't score a single goal in this game.

A sea of purple jerseys is making its way toward me as Revere's star player is dribbling the ball down the field. When it's finally kicked my way, I'm ready for it. I shield the kick with my body, and thwart (a vocab word, and a pretty cool way to say stop) their last chance to score.

The happy sounds of the Liberty fans who've come to watch fill the stands. Then the final buzzer sounds. The next thing I know, the girls on my team rush toward me. We're dancing on the field and jumping with our arms around each other.

Coach Newton blows her whistle. She's barreling toward us with a look on her face that says: *no excessive celebration*. At least not in front of the other team.

We disband and form a lineup to congratulate Revere. But as I fall into place behind Zoey and Callie and Emily, my mind wanders. It felt totally different to play in this game than it did the last. When our team played Brookside, it was so hard to focus on soccer. All I could think about was the election and Meghan and how we weren't friends anymore.

I glance up in the stands and see her sitting there. Next to Caleb. And the J's. Mom and Dad are there, too. And of course Ben. He's hard to miss because he's waving his arms like a crazy person.

"Way to go, Adams!" he shouts.

I give him a thumbs-up, then smile to myself.

It feels really good to know that all of the people I care about most are here to cheer me on. And even better that the election is behind me. And of course that I won! It's also nice to know I can get out on the field and have fun doing one of my favorite things. Which is playing soccer. For a while, I wasn't sure I'd ever enjoy it again.

But today I did a good job *and* had fun, too. That sounds soooo dramatic.

But it's not.

During the campaign, a lot of things got mixed up in my head. And I wasn't sure they'd ever get straightened out. I didn't think Meghan would ever be my best friend again. Or that my soccer team would forgive me for losing the game against Brookside. Or that Mom would get un-mad at me for promising something she hadn't agreed to.

Running a campaign was a lot harder than I thought it would be.

I guess the moral of the story is: do the best you can but know that there's a pretty good chance things might not go the way you expect them to. And sometimes that's a good thing, because in the end, things have a way of working themselves out.

Even when you're sure they won't.

I'm sure there's a French expression for all that. But I have no clue what it is.

Acknowledgments

I t takes a team to publish a book, and I'm one lucky author to be part of such an incredible group of people who brought this one together. First and foremost, huge thanks to my incredible editor, Allison Cohen. Your smarts and vision truly made *The Campaign* shine. To the rest of the team at Running Press Kids—most especially Michael Clark, Julie Matysik, Frances Soo Ping Chow, Valerie Howlett, Hannah Jones, and Mike McConnell—my most sincere gratitude for all of the hard work that you all put in to bring this book to life. Huge thanks to my agent, Susan Cohen, at PearlCo Literary Agency for all of your continued support, dedication, and smarts. To the real Amanda and Meghan—thanks so much for the inspiration! I hope you enjoy your fictional selves. And last but not least, my deepest thanks to all of the readers, librarians, booksellers, and media specialists out there. I hope you all love reading *The Campaign* as much as I enjoyed writing it.

L.B.F.